THREE GHOSTS
OF CHRISTMAS

ALSO BY DAVID RALPH WILLIAMS

GHOST STORIES

Olde Tudor

The Creaking Death

By a lantern's light

Dead Men's Eyes

Sacred – Ghostly Tales

The Christmas Room

ANTHOLOGIES

Icy creeps, gothic tales of terror

The Paranatural Detective Agency

THREE GHOSTS OF CHRISTMAS

By David Ralph Williams

Original cover illustration and design
by David Ralph Williams.
All other internal illustrations and
graphics were produced by the author
combined with Canva elements.

Thank you Cathy Start for the hard work put
into editing my manuscript. Your observations
and suggestions helped enormously.
I would like to thank you the reader for choosing this
little book amongst the multitudes of other titles
waiting to be discovered. I am forever thankful.

Three Ghosts
of
Christmas

Contents:

And think that I may never live to trace

*Their shadows with the magic
hand of chance.*

When I have fears that I may
cease to be – John Keats

THE SEAFORTH SILHOUETTES

Prelude

When my father passed away earlier this year, he left me a small independence of several hundred pounds per annum. This has allowed me to abandon my employ as a freelance journalist for one of the popular scandal sheets and pursue a career as a novelist. Novels are becoming fashionable and especially ghost stories from the likes of Dickens, who has demonstrated to be fearsomely adept at telling them. That notable author who pens in the genre seems largely concerned with such works of satirical fiction. I on the other hand would like to disclose a true and unsettling ghost story as told to me upon numerous occasions as a younger man when I had been a guest at my late uncle's house each Christmastide.

The following Christmas piece I aim to recount from memory with as much artistry as I can duly command. The tale harks back to former times of old when my Uncle Cedric would tell his much-loved story whenever encouraged to do so and without a pause. His listeners (including myself) would be enthralled as he spoke, and his gaze would never leave the guttering candles upon the chimneypiece where their dancing flames would reflect upon his faraway eyes. By the time he had finished telling his account it was as though he was thinking aloud to himself in an otherwise empty room. He would thereafter return from his reverie for the climax where he would then prove without *a shadow of a doubt* (no pun intended), the authenticity of his story.

THE SEAFORTH
SILHOUETTES

THE SEAFORTH
SILHOUETTES
I

That year's Yule log warmed the usual large accession of guests around the hearth at Seaforth Manor at Neyrock, Dorset. The house rested upon the towering white Breakneck Cliffs that stoop over the stacks and pinnacles sculpted by the crashing sea below. The Manor was the regnant toast of the locale and retained an overbearing feeling of antiquity. It occupied an isolated plot and one quite exposed and constantly battered by the elements. On approach, the house could appear ghostly especially when darkened by an oncoming storm brooding above the clifftops. It was even more so when the bitter sea winds shrieked, howled, and ruffled the great old elms that darkened the frontage allowing the windows to reflect the moonlight in a spectral manner.

That year's Christmas Eve dinner had been consumed, and the gathering of family and friends had moved from the eating parlour to a richly tapestried drawing room. It was a wing of the house that had been added much later but to all appearances, harmonised with the original construction perfectly. The current Lord of Seaforth Manor was Tobias Hinchcliffe, who inhabited the house along with his wife Olivia, daughter Rose, his dowager mother Christabel, and his younger brother Cedric. Joining the Hinchcliffes for that year's festivities were Gerald Creswell (Olivia's brother) and his wife Lucille, George Spencer and his wife Christina (Tobias's younger sister), and Clifford Emberton (Tobias's cousin).

The discussion after the meal had been concerned with the recent dismissal of a long-lasting servant by the name of Eve, whom Cedric had caught stealing food. It was late evening a fortnight since and he by chance happened to pass her on the servant's staircase whilst looking for his hound that had been missing since the afternoon. The pair almost bumped on the turn of the steps. Startled, Eve dropped the bundle she was carrying with her. Cedric apologised and went to retrieve the packet only to find the contents strewn about the lower steps.

Eve avoided eye contact with Cedric and roses bloomed upon her cheeks to pinken her aged face. She helped to pick up the assortment of edible foods that Cedric could see had undoubtedly been filched from the kitchens. She said she was on her way to dispose of the items claiming they had spoiled but Cedric could see how the bread and buns were newly baked and the venison at its best. The maid almost begged him not to speak of the matter to Tobias or Olivia and to calm her angst he told her that he would put the incident out of his mind.

"Lord bless you Sir!" she had said, before scurrying away sobbing lightly.

Cedric, unlike his brother, had from time to time concerned himself with the welfare of the servants at Seaforth. He wondered why Eve would need to take food from the kitchens and he concluded she had done so out of hunger. Worried that there may be an underlying problem amongst the maidservants, he was unable to keep his pledge to the woman and spoke of the matter with Tobias. The subject was taken up without any degree of sympathy by him who left the matter with Mrs Harding the housekeeper. She then dealt with the disciplinary measures that quickly saw Eve dismissed from service.

Eve claimed at the time that she had been taking the food to give to a relative who was not as fortunate as she.

"Theft is theft, whatever the reasons," said Lucille, as she sat playing whist with Olivia, Christina, and Christabel.

"I mean, do we not feed the servants at Seaforth?" replied Christabel coldly, who rarely displayed any emotion and had passed on these hard-hearted traits to her son Tobias. The whole unfortunate business had left Cedric feeling responsible for Eve's discharge and he wished he had kept his promise to the woman and not mentioned anything to his brother at all.

"I do feel terribly guilty about the whole affair. Eve had been with us for an awfully long time," confessed Cedric. His mother looked at him critically, tutting as she played her game taking the trick and placing the cards face down to one side on the table to be used later for scoring.

"Really Cedric, and I mean this in the most ardent terms, you do need to curb these emotive yearnings, it will be the undoing of you!" scolded Christabel but Cedric could not put his guilty conscience to one side. After Eve's dismissal he had checked with the other staff and Nora the cook had told him that she had gone to live with family. The news eased his mind a great deal considering her age and the general lack of opportunities in service for a woman of such mature years. He also knew that she had no hope of obtaining a good character testimonial from her one and only employers. Nora, the cook was the last to see her before she departed the house, and she claimed that Eve had singularly remarked, 'When I'm gone, I will pray for all of you.'

Feeling how the atmosphere required enlivening, Rose seated herself at the piano and performed a medley of Christmas carols much to the delight of everyone in the room. Tobias, perceptive to his daughter's motive glanced at the grandfather clock that had just declared the quarter past the hour and he used a bell-pull to summon his butler, Hubert. Tobias had organised a surprise guest to entertain the family but his visitor was late. When Hubert answered his master's call, Tobias was glad to hear that his guest had only just arrived and was warming himself by the fire in the great hall. Hubert explained how the weather had worsened during dinner and snow was now piling thick and heavy inland, carried from seaward squalls. Hubert left to fetch the man and almost toppled over Toddy, Cedric's Basset Hound as he scampered into the room.

On hearing the report on the weather, Clifford who had happily acted as Rose's page turner at the piano, moved over to a large Palladian window to observe the conditions for himself. His two years serving as a subaltern in the British army was almost over and he was about to be appointed captain of his regiment pending the approval of the colonel. He had attended the night's gathering sporting the livery of his junior ranking and Rose was, as ever, captivated by the young soldier in his scarlet coat and blue facings, white cross belt with silver plate, ruffled white chemise and black stock tie. She left the piano and came over to stand beside him as he cast his gaze upon a snow charmed winter's evening. Never taking her eyes off him, she studied his profile and his natural unpowdered youthful hair.

Clifford smiled when he saw Rose appear beside him; her expressive chestnut brown eyes told him all he needed to know about her feelings for him. It was no secret to the rest of the family and especially Christabel, that Rose and Clifford were fond of one another but Rose was still a young girl barely out of childhood yet budding into the woman she would soon become. In a year, she would make sixteen and she hoped then that Clifford would ask her for her hand. She was sure that her father would approve, as Clifford would be a captain in the British army by then and she had no doubt he would rise through the ranks due to his social standing. The enamoured pair watched as the snowflakes danced in the swirling air of the ever-whitening night.

"It looks so chilly, yet so beautiful," remarked Clifford. Rose touched his hand with a brush of her fingertips; the contact was noticed by Christabel as she procured another trick of the cards.

"The snowflakes look like goose feathers do they not?" posed Rose but Christabel muted Clifford's reply and bade the young pair to remove themselves from the window and resume the piano play.

"A house should hear music on a Christmas Eve," she added.

Just before Rose poised herself to recommence

play, Hubert's stout form reappeared at the doorway.

"Mr Styles Hemming Your Lordship," he announced. Toddy yapped at the tall stranger as he stepped into the room and bowed flamboyantly.

"It is a great honour my lords, ladies and gentlemen, to be invited to Seaforth tonight," boomed Hemming, "and near such a Holy day being the morrow of this Christmas Eve."

Tobias moved to greet the spindly guest who carried an assortment of belongings that he set down before shaking Tobias's hand. Toddy was still barking stridently forcing Cedric to quieten him.

The collection of family and friends all studied the new arrival and wondered who the odd - looking bespectacled silver-haired man was, or why he had been invited at all. As Tobias poured Hemming a brandy the man wandered about the room meeting each of the group in turn, offering his snuffbox to the men, whilst conducting a polite dally with the women. He deported himself as if he had access to the best society of the country. Tobias gave Hemming his drink before offering a formal introduction to the bemused cluster.

"I would like to present the celebrated Mr Styles Hemming, a leading artiste of our time and famous amongst the royal houses of Europe for his silhouette cutting. I asked him here so that he could perform his art for us all tonight," announced Tobias.

None of the family and friends had heard of the man but they all adored the stylish profile pictures that had become the fashion and remained so before the invention of photography would ultimately *overshadow* them.

"Oh, bravo Tobias," said Christabel, in appreciation of the enlivening forthcoming diversion. "Are you very good Mr Hemming," she enquired.

"May I be so bold as to proclaim that I am the best of my profession," he answered, depicting his self-grandeur.

"We shall be the judge of that," replied Christabel to her fellow card players, with a hushed tone.

Styles Hemming happily sat amongst the gathering whilst he clipped at his blackened French papers using a pair of sharpened steel scissors comprised of short blades with a special grip. Each cutting took him less than three minutes and was so delicate and miniature that it would fit inside a locket. Everyone who had had a likeness fashioned by Hemming was enchanted by the result. Tobias was the last to have his profile snipped and when Hemming had finished, he held it up between two of his slender fingers for the rest of the group to see. Olivia plucked it carefully from between Hemming's impeccably trimmed fingernails.

"Dearest, he has captured your prominent aquiline nose quite perfectly," she said, and passed the cutting around for others to review.

"He does have an amazing ability to bring such life to shadows," remarked Christina, before she then passed it back to Tobias.

Tobias looked at his own dark outline. His eyes beheld it, yet his thoughts were elsewhere. He broke his own reverie and pointed to the chimney breast above the lively fire.

"Of course! I have the answer Mother," he declared, and moved over to stand before the hearth-place. "You know how we discussed replacing these drear timeworn tapestries with something cheery?" he asked.

"I do," she agreed.

"Well, I've just had a rather splendid idea," said Tobias, and he went over to where Hemming was helping himself to another brandy.

"My dear fellow, having been so delighted by your work here tonight I would like to commission a further display of art to serve as a memento of this happy occasion."

Hemming offered Tobias his snuff box but he only wanted to convey to Hemming his latest impulse. Tobias described how he now wanted him to create a large genre picture in silhouette of the whole family as they engaged in their festive activities.

"I want everyone to be in it, including Toddy," said Tobias, pointing at Cedric's hound as it lay in the cosy light from the warm fire. "I want a scene big enough to cover the space upon the chimney piece left vacant after we remove that fusty old woollen remnant from my grandfather's time. Do you approve my dear?" he asked Olivia.

"I do, oh I do!" came her reply.

"Well Mother, do you like my notion?"

"I suppose I must agree to anything if it allows one to continue with their game of whist," replied Christabel.

"Then it is settled, and I promise to pay quite handsomely. Sir, would you take up this contract?" Hemming weighed up the space presently taken by the tapestry.

"I will sir. I have done a similar piece that now hangs in the New Palace in Potsdam, Prussia. King Friedrich of course engaged me himself," he said proudly.

Tobias picked up the brandy decanter and walked about the room topping up the empty glasses of his family and finally Hemming's vacant cognac tumbler.

"Then we shall moisten our pallets sir. All you need to do is observe us at play and cut away on your papers."

Tobias gathered his family around a larger Gentleman's Social Table for games of *fire dragon*, and *charades*. Hemming at one point produced a large sheet from one of his personal travelling bags. Hubert was called for, and with his help, the sheet was hung between Hemming and the family so that a lamp projected the shadows of the revelry upon it. This projection created an aid for Hemming's work. Hubert was afterwards detained by the family who insisted that he too must be in the picture.

The Manor was the regnant toast of the locale and retained an overbearing feeling of antiquity. It occupied an isolated plot and one quite exposed and constantly battered by the elements.

The hour had become late. The family had gradually withdrawn themselves from all forms of gaiety to sit fatigued before the fire that had now reduced to a rosy glow of embers. Styles Hemming packed away his accoutrements stating that he was pleased with the results.

"I shall take my cuttings with me and arrange them artistically as you requested. The finished piece shall be delivered within the week," he explained. Tobias thanked him.

"Surely you cannot travel back in such conditions?" said Olivia, alluding to the weather.

"You are right my dear, Mr Hemming can stay at Seaforth tonight. I shall call a maid to make up a room," said Tobias but Hemming stopped him before he used the bell rope.

"Your hospitality has been most gracious but I could not impose upon a family on Christmas morning, no. I do have an invitation to spend the festive season with members of my extended family who dwell in a nearby town and not too far away from Seaforth. They are eager to have me stay with them on account of my growing prominence," replied Hemming. "My driver I believe, waits in the kitchens."

"As you wish but instruct your driver to keep well away from the 'Landless Road' to Old Nick's Point; the snow would make that a perilous journey, and we would not want any accidents," warned Tobias.

"I shall heed your words sir and will pass on your sound advice to my driver," said Hemming, before bidding his farewells.

II

Christmas at Seaforth came and went and all those within saw in the New Year merrily. The family had planned to stay in residence up to Twelfth Night as was the custom for the Hinchcliffes. The only exception being Clifford, who had braved the weather to return to his regiment on time, where he was to be posted to Malta in preparation for the much-anticipated peace treaty that would be signed in Amiens. Rose missed him dearly and she hoped that he was right when he had told her that after the signing of the treaty there would hopefully follow peace in Europe from Bonaparte's army. Clifford had learned that the British planned to withdraw from Malta before handing it back to the Order of St. John of Jerusalem, with its neutrality guaranteed by the nations.

The snow had remained as a thick mantle swathing the land and it was only by Twelfth Night that it had started to thaw but a sharp dip in temperature had then turned the snow into dangerous sheets of ice. The inclemency of the weather forced all to remain at the house, venturing out only to attend the customary church services. The coach would constantly lose traction and the men would have to periodically dig around the wheels to free them, and as they toiled, the horses' breath would hang about them in the hardened air.

The prolonged harsh weather saw the family stay together at Seaforth longer than in previous years. One morning Gerald and Lucille, and George and Cedric wrapped in winter apparel all ventured outside to assess the conditions. Cedric brought his hound, and they took the 'Landless Road' to Old Nick's Point. At one spot about midway down the trail all of them slipped to fall bottomward upon the glassy ice. Toddy was the only one who managed to stay upright on all four of his legs whilst the rest struggled to get on their feet bringing hilarity to the group as they tottered about trying to keep each other upright upon the frozen road.

Eventually, and with much mirth, they made it to Old Nick's Point where they stood on the cliff top rocked by a raw wind, and the howling air stirred the stiff wild grasses in a percussion of rattling. The white towers of rock with their iced topping now resembled a vast glacial ice shelf.

"This place always frightens me," shouted Lucille, as she tried to prevent the wind from stealing her words and the large plume fixed to her bonnet.

"There is nothing to be frightened of. We

should respect but not fear the elements," Gerald responded.

"Indeed, such places serve to motivate us to make sense of the world around us," added George. Lucille crouched to safely look over the precipice where she watched the ebb and flow of the rhythmic beat of the sea and the well-whipped brine as it crashed against the talus piles below.

"I say Lucille, do not look over such a height, it may cause a *gal* to cast up one's accounts!" Gerald quipped.

"Do not worry Gerry, I have a strong enough stomach for heights. I do feel afraid though whenever I come here. I cannot explain my intuitions but it is not the elements I fear, more so the elementals."

"Elementals? Come now dearest, all this talk is claptrap. You know how you have always suffered a touch of the *blue devils* this time of year," derided Gerald, before walking off with Toddy who was scampering at his heels to explore a nearby escarpment. Lucille cast Gerald a hostile glance as he went away. George offered her a hand up and Cedric noticed how their hands remained connected far beyond the time needed to facilitate Lucille's balance.

"I think you might be right; I always feel that the natural world offers a sort of divine connection and can stir one's belief in the supernatural and may I say, elementals dear

Lucille," said George, as the wind riffled through his carroty hair and he released her hand when the pair of them saw how Cedric had noted their improper familiarity. For a moment, all three turned to watch Gerald who seemed so far away now as he poked about in the ice with a stick he had found.

"Olivia once told me a most unpleasant story of how a servant at Seaforth fell to their death exactly where we are now!" said George, to break the awkward silence that had developed.

"How awful. Is it true Cedric?" asked Lucille.

"It was a very long time ago," replied Cedric.

"Then it is true. Oh, how horrible. Please tell the story," Lucille insisted.

"I hardly know it. It happened before I was born. It was a stable boy I think."

"The poor fellow fell to his death and drowned in the sea below," added George.

"The story I know is that the boy was caught up on a ledge that used to jut out quite near the bottom before it collapsed into the sea some years later. I remember being told that he was winched up and brought back to Seaforth where he died much later but I am not wholly certain. Only Granny or Hubert would know for sure."

"No wonder it is named Old Nick's Point," said George glumly.

The biting gusts saw all four take the icy road

back to Seaforth. Once back home the group had decided that they would ask Nora the cook to prepare them all a hot flannel of gin, beer, and nutmeg to warm them up. As the house loomed before them, they saw a carriage leaving the manor and the walkers carefully left the road so that the trap could pass by. George questioned who would call at the house in such conditions. None of them could think of a reason as nobody was expected.

As they walked through the manor gateway, the house, still hugged by the recent snowfalls and hard frost, resembled a white castle. The great elms now unclothed carried upon their boughs the icicle gems of such wintery days, and they glittered in the fading sunlight. A twig-armed snowman greeted them near the entrance as a reminder of recent family recreation.

When they had collected their hot drinks from the kitchen, they made their way to the drawing room intending to spend the rest of the afternoon seated before the fire and dosing in the ever-encroaching twilight. Their plans were quickly forgotten however when they discovered that Hemming's silhouette picture had arrived, and they now had an answer to the mysterious carriage that they had seen leaving the house. Tobias and Hubert were busy hanging the picture upon the chimney piece whilst Christabel, Olivia, Rose, and Christina all stood waiting in anticipation to view it in position. Once in place

Hubert collected up all the cloths and string that had wrapped it.

"Will there be anything else Your Lordship?" he asked.

"No, that will be all Hubert thank you," replied Tobias, and Hubert went about his other duties. Tobias was happy to see the returning members of the family so that he could show off his picture. "Well, I think it looks rather splendid do you not agree?"

Everyone gathered before the picture and Christabel produced a pair of eyeglasses to study the formation of fabricated shadows captured within a gilded Baroque style frame.

"Goodness am I really so plump?" remarked Christabel, as she studied her own outline in the picture. Nobody dared answer her remark and Rose commented that she could guess who everyone was bar one exception. She pointed to a shorter figure, youth sized, standing apart from the rest as though quietly monitoring them. Each of them studied the figure but none were able to provide an explanation of who it was intended to be, as everyone else in the picture could be accounted for including Hubert and Toddy.

"Perhaps one of the other servants? We were all so distracted in our games to have noticed," suggested Tobias.

"You must be right Papa," answered Rose. "Yes, that must be it. I think it could be Pippa or Ted."

"My dear girl, it is most definitely not Pippa.

Can you not see that the figure is wearing knee breeches!" snapped Christabel.

"Oh, you are right Granny I see that now."

"I am right, and I shall settle this by calling for Hubert. One's butler should always know what the rest of the servants are doing. I am sure he will remember."

Christabel rang for him before returning to her chair.

Hubert arrived carrying a carafe of port, believing the reason for his call was so the family could indulge themselves earlier than was usual in the ruby after-dinner wine most appropriate during chilly weather. Still carrying the flask, Tobias guided him over to the silhouette picture and then asked his opinion on the unidentified figure.

"We each have our own theory as to whom it might be but there is a lack of consensus to all the claims. We rather hoped that you might be able to shed some light on the matter," said Tobias. Hubert nodded his understanding and peered at the picture. Tobias offered his eyeglasses but Hubert took a step back. His jaw fell as he stared ahead in abject horror as though taking fright from it and he seemed to stagger. The port he was holding slipped from his grasp but was rescued by Tobias's quick reflexes.

"I am sorry Your Lordship," he apologised almost collapsing, "Perhaps I am coming down with a chill."

"Goodness, help the poor man to a chair Tobias," said Christabel.

"Thank you, My Lady but I shall be quite alright, yes quite alright in a moment," he said as his pallid face now became flushed.

"Perhaps you should relieve yourself of your duties for the rest of the evening Hubert, after all, none of us are getting any younger," said Christabel. Hubert nodded and mopped his brow with a handkerchief. He quickly departed the room after casting a nervous glance back at the framed picture.

The following morning the family were eating breakfast together all except Rose as she could never manage to consume a morsel before noon. It was Hubert who brought good tidings to the breakfast table. According to him, the recent ice covering the roads in a perilous shell had actually thawed. The melt was now sufficient to allow those who had remained at Seaforth longer than intended to plan their departure.

"We could share a coach to Bridport," said Christina, "and then Gerry and Lucille can carry on to Blandford."

George agreed because he knew it was in vain to do anything else.

"Then it is settled, we shall head off tomorrow after spending one final night at Seaforth," said Gerald.

"Sister, may I have Pippa help me to pack my things?" asked Christina.

"Yes of course," Olivia replied.

"I shall need a valet, Tobias, may I purloin yours?" asked Gerald.

"Indeed. I shall make Stanley aware. Before you all leave, I would like to suggest that we have a special dinner tonight; the house will seem rather empty when you have all abandoned us," said Tobias.

"That is a nice idea Tobias," said Christabel, "and before you all go, we could have one final game of whist!"

Later that afternoon Rose sat quietly in the drawing room as she penned a letter to Clifford. It was her intention to write to him in Malta every week until they could be reunited. She would ensure that the letters were delivered to the packet ship by horse post and was sure that Clifford would be appreciative enough to pay to receive them.

When she had finished her letter, she folded it inside another sheet of paper with a lock of her chestnut hair and sealed it with a piece of wax. The act of writing to Clifford had excited her as she tried to imagine his face as he read her tender words. Now she was finished she felt bereft from the happiness the act of writing to her love had given her. She stood alone in the room and moved across to the hearth where the silhouette picture hung. The clock said three in its usual peal, and she stood on her toes so she could see the black profile of Clifford as he had stood that Christmas Eve at her shoulder at the piano, the whole moment captured by Hemming so strikingly.

She blinked and then rubbed at her eyes when she noticed that the small figure that had caused much discussion and conjecture amongst them the previous day had appeared to have been displaced. She was sure that the *unknown youth* had originally been positioned away from the family, yet here now he was standing beside the chair upon which the outline of her grandmother sat. She blinked again because the borders of the cutting seemed to blur as though she could not focus her eyes upon it with any precision. There was another thing too; the figure was in a different posture to how she had remembered it.

"Papa! Mama!" called Rose, when she found Tobias and Olivia reading in the mahogany library. Both of them almost dropped their books when she came dashing into the room.

"What on earth is wrong my dear," asked Olivia, concerned that a household emergency had gone unnoticed by them both.

"The odd silhouette who none of us could put a name to has moved in your picture Papa."

"Nonsense my dear," replied Tobias in disbelief.

"It has, it really has, come and see!" Rose said, almost begging them both to follow her through to the drawing room.

Tobias stood opposite the framed scene staring intensely at the area where Rose pointed her finger. If he was honest, he thought the scene looked exactly as he remembered it.

"The figure has crossed half the room to stand beside Granny. You must see it Papa?"

Tobias shook his head. "I am sorry Rose; I simply do not remember but pictures do not move by themselves. Is it possible you were mistaken my dear?"

"I am not mistaken Papa, I distinctly recall the figure to be standing on the other side here," she said, indicating a vacant space that now put the whole scene out of balance. Tobias just shook his head and turned to Olivia.

"Do you remember anything different about this picture my dear?"

Olivia joined her daughter and her husband. Rose was still pointing to the empty space.

"I think I do remember a figure to be standing slightly away from the rest of us but how can I?"

"Thank you, Mama, now I know that I am not losing my senses. It *has* moved, you can see that it has."

"Perhaps there is someone at the house open to practical jokes?" Olivia speculated.

III

Dinner had been served and consumed early that evening to give the whole family more time for some final social relations. Christabel played whist with Lucille, Olivia, and Christina. Rose was discussing the silhouette picture with Cedric and was imparting to him the latest bewildering discovery about it. Cedric had to confess to not noticing the change in the picture and the others in the room paid no notice to Rose's constant chatter about it, believing that she was using the whole episode as a distraction to plug a void left by Clifford's departure to his regiment.

Rose returned to her chair and sank down into it, frustrated that none of her family was the least bit interested in the displaced silhouette cutting. She had been overstimulated by the Christmas festivities and now she was bored. She watched and wondered how the rest of her family could find so much contentment in diversions such as smoking, or card games. She studied Christabel as she played whist, her whole countenance shone of cheerfulness, such pleasure derived from the simple game.

It was whilst observing the ongoing card play that Rose noticed how her grandmother had suddenly become rigid, sitting in her chair like a statue. Rose saw what looked like a black puddle beneath her feet and it seemed to almost grow up around her, embracing her with sleek and fluid arms. No one else appeared to notice as all eyes were fixed upon the cards and the glasses of rubicund wine, and the haze of tobacco curls, yet Rose continued to watch as her grandmother's skin took on the appearance of sooty streaks muting her natural colour.

Christabel released her hand of cards and one side of her face dropped as though caught by an invisible hook and line.

"Granny!" screamed Rose, and leapt out of her seat to attend to her grandmother. She was followed by the rest of the family who had now noticed Christabel's sudden transformation. Olivia reached across the card table to steady her as she began to slip sideways from her chair.

"Mama, what is wrong," called Tobias, who repositioned her in the chair. Christabel said nothing yet she gagged in an unpleasant fashion. Rose noticed how the black daubs that had darkened her face only moments ago had now receded. Her eyes, moist and vacant, just stared ahead not seeing any of the worried faces around her. Cedric used a bell rope to summon a servant.

"We should call for a physician at once," he

said, and joined his brother still propping up their mother. Moments later Hubert entered the room and seeing the emergency unfolding before him he quickly crossed the floor to help. Hubert was sent away with orders to fetch for the doctor without delay.

"We need to get Mama to her bed, I fear she has suffered an attack of some sort," said Tobias, and both he and Cedric lifted her up from the chair and together they carried her out of the room and up to her bedchamber.

She pointed to a shorter figure, youth sized, standing apart from the rest as though quietly monitoring them.

The doctor arrived at Seaforth so quickly it was as though the Devil's own coachman had driven him. Sadly, by the time he had been taken to Christabel's chamber, she had already passed. The whole family was at her bedside as she lay corpse-still. Everyone at Seaforth was bereft; Dorothy, Christabel's personal maid wept desolately. The doctor apologised saying he came as fast as he was able.

"From the description you gave me of her preceding condition, I can only conclude that your dear departed mother had suffered an apoplexy, a bleeding of the brain," explained the doctor to Tobias and Cedric.

"What do you suppose could have triggered it?" asked Cedric, who was now visibly suffering from the shock of the ordeal.

"Her age more than anything else, although I had been treating Lady Hinchcliffe for an aberrant heartbeat for quite some time, ever since the death of your father as it happens," the doctor answered.

Rose listened to all the talk within the room and watched as Dorothy tenderly drew the bedcurtains around her old mistress. Rose remembered what she had seen moments before her grandmother took ill. She thought about it but kept all her notions to herself. She was certain though that it had something to do with the silhouette of the unknown boy that had inexplicably moved within the picture to stand beside Christabel's own dark contour.

"We cannot possibly leave Seaforth now," said Christina.

"I agree, we shall stay in residence until after the funeral," added George.

"Gerry and I will also stay and help you with the arrangements," piped Lucille. Gerald grimaced knowing all too well how much time he had already spent with his in-laws.

"Of course, let us know what we can do to help," Gerald then added graciously. Lucille smiled at George who reciprocated briefly because he knew in that moment, gladness for any sake was not appropriate.

It had been Christabel's wish that her funeral ought to be arranged by the same furnisher as had been used for the burial of her husband. The whole ceremonious ritual from the vigil to the burial and service itself was planned, and no expense was spared for any part of the funeral as the whole family felt obliged to do all they could to honour their much-loved mother and grandmother. Tobias and Cedric were given a schedule of all the arrangements for a funeral appropriate for a family of such standing. Once everything on the list was approved by Tobias, Seaforth became occupied by members of the furnisher's employ.

First, a pair of women washed, dressed, and prepared Christabel's body for placement in the coffin. The coffin was constructed out of the finest planks of knot-free elm and lined with an ivory woven taffeta. A silver breast plate was fastened to the lid engraved with Christabel's name and date of death. One room at Seaforth had been fully draped in black cloth for the *lying-in-repose* before the burial. During the repose vigil, the room had been illuminated by candles and Christabel's coffin was watched over by professional *watchers* of the furnisher's employ, whilst the draping of the church and the organising of the vehicle for the funeral procession was arranged.

***

The unhappy morning finally landed at Seaforth and the family were waiting for the funeral furnisher and his entourage to arrive. Black cloaks over suits were worn by all the male members of the family and black crêpe gowns by the women. Cedric stood at the front entrance along with the rest of the family and servants as the funeral coach was drawn slowly up the path towards the house. He saw how elegant the Belgian Blacks looked wearing their funerary harnesses and black ostrich plume head-dresses and it brought back memories of his father's funeral as the horses pulled the coach behind them, the pulsing sound of metal shoe upon gravel. The mutes, bearers and pages, all properly dressed by the furnisher in their gowns, sashes, hatbands, and gloves carried staves as they walked with a methodical tread unspeaking like black swans that dreamily float by so silently.

Rose joined her parents in waiting as the six bearers opened the coach in preparation for its load then entered the house to collect the coffin.

She thought how odd it was that the whole scene before her now resembled a picture like the one created by Hemming in which she and everyone else apart from her grandmother were now living silhouettes. The coffin had been covered in black silk fastened by brass nails. As it was brought out of the house the horses stood stock-still, a breed known for their calm temperament, as the coffin was loaded onto the coach.

It was the gloomiest morning that a January could bring, and rain began sheeting upon the clifftops as the convoy of carriages slowly rolled along the winding lane that led to the church. The churchyard was never an appealing sight even in summertime and that morning a number of dark crows that tended to linger about the place provided yet an even more baleful mood. The family dismounted the coaches to the ringing of the knells as a clergyman emerged from the church carrying a prayerbook. Christabel's coffin remained covered by the silken cloth until it reached the graveside. Once all were stood around the open cavity the formal rituals began.

Many from the local villages came to pay their respects. Cedric noticed that Eve was standing next to an aged cottager and his wife. News of Christabel's passing must have reached her, and she had felt obliged to attend the service but was keeping her distance because of the shame of her dismissal. Cedric wanted to go over and tell her that she need not stay away but should join the other servants in attendance but then the reading of a biblical text began followed by the casting of soil by each family member onto the casket.

"Man and woman came from the earth, and so must they return to earth," said the vicar solemnly. When Cedric looked up, Eve had gone.

Eve was standing next to an aged cottager and his wife. News of Christabel's passing must have reached her, and she had felt obliged to attend the service but was keeping her distance because of the shame of her dismissal.

The wake had been held at Seaforth and had lasted the customary four days. Gerald was once more itching to depart from the house and the doleful atmosphere that had enveloped it. Plans were again made for a coach to take both George and Christina, and Gerald and Lucille to Bridport.

The whole family did not seem to know what to do with themselves. The small table where Christabel had last sat and played whist remained as it was, enshrined with all the cards still spread upon it. Even Toddy seemed out of sorts, and he grew into a nervous dog, barking and whimpering at empty doorways and corners, as though he was trying to deter menaces that were indiscernible to the rest of the family.

Post was delivered to the house and with it came a letter addressed to Rose. Hubert delivered it and Rose could see that it was from Clifford's regiment as it bore the mark and was addressed in Clifford's hand. Pleased that he had written to her she stole away to her bedchamber to read his words in private.

IV

The next part of the story shall be told by Clifford Emberton in the form of the letter received by Rose. The missive was a private communication betwixt a pair of beloveds and the private nature of some of the content will be omitted for the sake of respectability. I have kept the letter in my possession to this very day since it was handed to me by my late uncle Cedric when he learned about my intention of writing an account of the story of which he was the only living source. The next words will be those of Clifford. Some names of his comrades and those of higher military rank will be excluded for the protection of their families and descendants.

I write to thee my dearest Rose and yearn once again to be in your company. I am myself a good deal indisposed as I wait for my regiment's leave from Malta, and I will endeavour to explain why I feel so assailed and why the tone of this letter is so cheerless. As you know I have served over two years as a subaltern in the army after my father purchased my original commission before another most recent imbursement to see me appointed to captain. Only the colonel himself can approve such an advancement but before he can do so, he must take recommendations from my immediate superior officer who would weigh such testimonials against my education, physical vigour, and overall stability of character for one to assume leadership of men. I have of late failed to impress upon my own superior Captain M— for the reasons I will now reveal but please my darling, do not think of me as crazed, I am of sound mind as you know and have always known.

The whole battalion had been quartered in the Maltese countryside so that we could feed our horses. Our barracks were converted barns and stables where men slept side by side upon makeshift straw beds, some of higher rank had benches. These conditions concerned me not, for as soldiers we have known much worse.

My main comrade J— whom I have known since boyhood and had joined the ranks at the same time as I, always slept by my side, and over time I was glad of his nearness because I have always been a light sleeper and during those nights in the barn I would lie upon the straw listening to the stertor of the men, and our dogs and horses, and the hooters in the trees outside and these sounds were almost a comfort. You see, the lamps were always turned to low wick at night and the shadows of the horses would bruise the bents and bays of the barn but there was another shadow within the space not cast from a cavalry charger.

I would rise on my elbows and watch it creep and clamber over the sleeping men as it always made a course to where I lay. I feel there is something about the shadow that is conscious, alive, and vaguely satanic. It is a loathsome sight. I would always wake my sleeping comrade and make him look for the shadow but whenever he did, it would always remain hidden in the dead darkness. It goes without saying that J— soon tired of these nightly disturbances at my hand and I was forced to use money to buy myself a room at a local tavern where my own superior, Captain M— was quartered.

The change of board did not see an improvement in the situation. Try as I might to keep my mind detached from fancy, I continued to see the dark apparition as I drank ale in the tavern after supper. The firelight would always create shadows of its own, yet I would seek out the one that did not fit, the one without a body to cast it. It was a diminutive shape and sometimes headless. I would watch in fear as it crept ever slowly towards where I sat. Blooms of winter wild fennel jugged upon the tables would decay as soon as its shade darkened them.

I would immediately leave the tavern and walk the night away staying close to the maisonettes and solitary farmhouses bathed in the protective tallow light from the windows. I would wonder as I walked as to the nature of the ghost, yes Rose, for a ghost is what it must surely be. Was the shadow hunting me that of a man I once killed in battle, who died on my sword? Was it a thing that had never seen heaven's gate, a thing that now echoes through a world that has become a gaol for its soul? I realised that I could not continue this way as lack of rest would only lead to sickness or far worse. I broached the subject with J — and begged him to spend a night in my bedchamber at the tavern. Mercifully, he agreed.

That night we both sat up late with a bottle of rum between us as I told him my troubles and he was a great comfort, lightening my mood. His answer had been that we should speak with a ghost that wandered into our presence. I knew that a spirit seeking answers to its own pains could not find its solutions from the two of us. If indeed it was the ghost of a man I had once slew, then that help I could not give because I have learned that in the battles of men there are no real answers. The rum brought swift sleep for both of us but as my head lay pillowed, the part of my soul that never slept knew I was in mortal danger. I woke in the early hours to find the spirit mounting the bed on which I lay. I shouted in terror at this dark thing and before all firmness forsook me, I reached under my pillow for my barking irons and fired directly at it. When the smoke had cleared, I saw J— lying dead on the floor, his gore pooling about him, two pistol wounds in his breast.

I was marched before my superiors and in particular, Major T—. The major bawled at me, his sun-browned face turning almost burgundy. I was so fatigued I could not even comprehend what words the major expectorated in my general direction. All I could do was observe his glare beneath his scarce hair and soon I was marched out of his presence and cast into temporary imprisonment. They now believe I have contracted a serious form of brain fever, and at the request of Captain M— I am now moved to a hospital for recuperation. If I were of lesser social standing, I fear I would have been shot or hung but the death of my friend at my hand is punishment enough. Perhaps I am ill, for as I write this letter to you my dearest Rose, I can see the spirit outside my window each nightfall as it waits for me. If this spirit is just a symptom of an illness, then I shall fear it no longer and wait for my health to return and the spirit to wane.

Oh, how I long for the time I can join you at Seaforth again where once we sat contented underneath the spreading arms of the old elms.

As ever very sincerely yours

Clifford

V

Still clutching Clifford's letter, Rose hurried through the warren of dark oaken panelled rooms until she reached the drawing room. There were only two portraits of Christabel at Seaforth, and both had been brushed in oils when she had been a young woman. As was the custom, her portraits had been draped in mourning lace. The most recent likeness of her, captured by Hemming using his black French paper had also been covered. She stood before the veiled silhouette picture and gingerly lifted the lace. She inhaled sharply and stepped back from the picture as Toddy scampered into the room followed by Cedric.

Cedric could see that Rose was shaken; her whole demeanour exhibited profound dread. He asked her what was wrong, and she thrust Clifford's letter into his hand. He scanned the writing and although Clifford's words were brooding and carried with them a sense of fear, he just looked at his niece for an explanation of her sudden anxiety.

"The picture Uncle, it has moved again come

and look!" she cried, as her voice fractured under her distress. She parted the lace for him to see. As he studied the picture his eyes grew wide, and his complexion paled, and she knew that he too could see.

"I worry for Clifford, his words are so gloomy, and I can't forget what happened to Granny," she said, now trembling.

"My mother died of apoplexy, you heard what the doctor said. She was old, and time had caught up with her," Cedric reminded Rose.

"Oh, but surely you remember how the silhouette of the nameless figure had moved. You must recall examining the picture to see how the figure had repositioned itself to be near to Granny before she suffered her fit or whatever it was the doctor said. Now look again Uncle, for the picture has once more altered. That worrying figure has crossed the room to be near Clifford."

Cedric could see that the scene had changed but he had no explanation for the alteration.

"Rose, how can a piece of paper move untouched by earthly hands? What you are suggesting is grotesquely fanciful!"

"I know Uncle, yet it *has* happened, we both know it has."

As Rose spoke, she studied the shape of the nameless shadow. She noticed how its outline was not as crisp as the other profiles in the picture; it seemed slightly ill-defined and blurred and no amount of focussing of the eyes could bring it into clarity.

"I feel that there is a flowing of a soul in that youthful silhouette, yet only the darkest parts of it remain. I must warn Clifford, I must write to him at once," she said, before departing for her bedchamber.

The conversation that evening was about the picture. Dinner was concluded early and before dessert course so that everyone could see for themselves the nature of the silhouette's transformation. With the lace now completely removed the whole family were aghast as they stood before the picture, all of them unable to explain the phenomenon that presented itself before them. Cedric and Rose exchanged surprised glances for the scene had shifted once again. The irregular figure had now left Clifford's side to lurk close to George's likeness.

"It has to be some clever deception, yes that must be it," said Tobias, "Hemming is an artist of the highest level, he creates works for royalty. His skill must involve some form of conjuring, an illusion of some sort."

"*Witching* more like," added Rose under her breath but not so quiet that Cedric did not hear.

"By Jove, I think you have it Tobias," said Gerald.

"I do, I am sure of it. Why, it must add to the allure, providing him with even more commissions. We just do not know how the mechanism works," said Tobias, as he scrutinised the frame.

"Like one of those clocks with the moving figures?" added Olivia.

"Exactly my dear. I shall dispatch a letter in the morning to Hemming himself asking for his affirmations."

Rose was not swallowing her father's explanation, choosing instead to believe that the picture held within its borders an embodiment of something sinister.

"So, I have nothing to worry about at all," laughed George, after Rose had earlier spelled out the consequences of having the changeable and nameless silhouette pairing with his own.

"I suggest we all forget about the picture for we have at last hit upon its secrets," said Tobias, and everyone dispersed from the chimney piece to set about their usual evening rituals.

Rose drew a chair close to the fire for she intended to sit and to keep her gaze firmly upon the picture. It was a fact that the features within it or rather one in particular, had a life of its own and she was determined to catch the moment where it redeployed itself. Cedric failed to persuade her otherwise and so she sat, and she waited as the clock on the mantle sang the divisions of the hours. She hoped that her father was right and that it was only a clever trick built into the picture by Hemming himself. If she saw it move with a clockwork motion then she could stop thinking about how her grandmother had looked as she crumpled and shrunk in her chair. She could also stop worrying about Clifford, and about George and put the whole ghastly notion out of her mind before it became unspooled by the flowing outlines of black that had little by little infected it.

"Rose, everyone has turned in for the night, I think it is time to call it a day."

Rose opened her eyes to find Cedric standing over her. The warmth of the fire had made her sleepy. She rubbed at her eyes and glanced at the picture. No change had occurred; the nameless silhouette was still positioned next to George.

"You cannot sit here all night," he said, as she picked up a candlestick and held it before the picture establishing the fact that no movement had occurred.

"It has been a long day Uncle, so I will bid you goodnight," she said, before departing for bed.

Sleep was disturbed in the small hours by screaming that exuded from George and Christina's room. A bell rope had brought servants scampering to the bedchamber door and due to the clamour from within, polite etiquette was abandoned, and the door was forced open. The scene that greeted the servants and family, who were subsequently roused from sleep, was an awful one.

Within the room, Christina had shrunk to a corner and was pointing to George's sprawled form upturned over the bed end. His head was down to the floor and in his hand, he clutched a fire-hook. There was a line of blood oozing from his bottom lip bitten during his agony, his eyes protruded dreadfully, and his face wore a grimace of terror. George was clearly quite dead. A sheet was quickly pulled over his body and the women ushered out of the room. Hubert and Tobias put a robe around Lucille before guiding her quaking form out of the room and down to the drawing room where a fire was lit.

It was almost dawn when the doctor called to examined George's body upstairs. Lucille was grief-stricken by the whole affair. Gerald tried unsuccessfully to pacify her but she withdrew to her bedchamber. The family was given an account of the terrible event by Christina, her nerves at this point were deadened by brandy.

"George woke me, and he was acting in a wild and fevered manner. He said that he was sure an animal had got into our room and that the alleged beast was under the bed!" said Christina.

"An animal. What kind of animal?" queried Tobias.

"I do not know for I never saw it but George was adamant that we were in danger from whatever he believed he had seen. He told me not to move before he sprang off the bed to arm himself with the fire iron. When he attempted to clamber back atop the coverlets, he screamed in panic saying that *it had his feet*, and it was as though he was fastened to the floor and it took all his strength to make it back atop the bed but then he cried out in agony clutching his chest, and I saw … saw—"

"Saw what," asked Rose, now so troubled she appeared ashen.

"I am not sure, a patch of shadow, nothing more. It was then George started fitting and I began screaming. I thought he was going to strike me with the fire iron, so I ran to the corner and watched as he began to briefly tussle with what appeared to be an imaginary assailant."

Christina threw back her head and began to giggle nervously, her laughter quickly turning to tears. Tobias took the brandy out of his sister's hand and gave it to Cedric to hold.

"She is in shock, and quite *jug bitten*. I will ask the doctor if he has a sleeping draft," said Tobias and left the room. Christina asked Cedric for more brandy but he refused. Tobias returned with the doctor who administered her with a tincture of opium before she was put to bed.

The doctor's conclusion was that George died of *Anger in the chest*, causing an arrest of the heart resulting in his sudden death. Rose was sceptical of the diagnosis and echoed her belief that the silhouette picture was linked to her uncle's death. Nobody paid attention to her views as all were feeling too distraught by the whole incident.

***

George's funeral took place near his family parish at Bridport and another period of mourning began. Christina remained at her home in Bridport after deciding she could not return to Seaforth. Lucille and Gerald maintained their residence throughout the new period of bereavement. For Lucille, the loss of George had brought much sorrow and during breakfast one morning her display of sadness was such that Gerald was induced to speak his mind.

"I do wonder Lucille if you would be so heartbroken if it had been I who had departed this world," he remarked. Gerald's brusque words saw Lucille make her excuses and remove herself from the breakfast table, the tears in her soul once more breaking through to brim in her eyes. Cedric drained the coffee from his cup and together with Toddy, who had sat patiently at his feet, went away in search of Lucille.

He found her quietly sobbing in the solarium. When she saw him, she wiped at her eyes using a small handkerchief which she kept up her sleeve.

"I think I understand the extent of the grief you try so hard to conceal," said Cedric, as Toddy went to her, tail wagging. She bent to fuss him and took his paw in her hand.

"George was ... a dear friend," she said.

Cedric had come to his own conclusions over

time regarding George and Lucille's fondness for one another but had said nothing of it. He pondered if Gerald was also aware.

"Do you think there is any truth in what Rose says when she speaks about the silhouette picture somehow being responsible for all the blackness that has befallen Seaforth of late?" Lucille asked him. Cedric sat down in a chair opposite to consider her question.

"I think Rose's beliefs are a product of her own fancy and overexcited nerves. We cannot surely believe ourselves haunted by a malicious spectre cast from an image?"

"I am not so sure Cedric; you see I have also seen such portents of late."

"What are you referring to?"

"Just flickers, perhaps a patch of shadow from the corner of my eye, here and there."

Cedric felt a superstitious fear creep over him.

"Tobias said he would contact the man who fashioned the picture. I am sure that it will bring an end to all our speculations about it."

"I do hope you are right Cedric, really I do."

It was an overcast afternoon and despite the prospect of rain, Rose had opted to remove herself from the heavy atmosphere within the house and take a walk upon the clifftops. The wintry wind was blowing the graphite grey clouds that had gathered overhead into artistic swirls. Light rain began to spot the ragged tussocks underfoot bringing out their colours and leaving liquid orb gems upon the blades. When the spots of rain fell heavier, she decided to return back home before the deluge commenced. Thunder began to grumble like a battalion's drumroll. She picked up her pace and then heard the sound of a carriage approaching from behind. The carriage passed her and as it did, she caught a glimpse of a ruby-red coat from inside. Immediately it felt as though her ribs had transformed to become like the rigid bars of a birdcage and her heart a snared fowl within. It had to be Clifford in the carriage, he had returned from the wars like he had promised.

Lifting up her crinoline dress, Rose ran to follow the carriage that had now rested in front of the house. She could hardly contain her excitement at the prospect of a reunion with Clifford. The door of the carriage opened, and a figure dropped to the ground.

"Clifford," called Rose, and the man donning the apparel of a soldier in Clifford's regiment turned to greet her. Immediately she could see that it was not Clifford but another man, similar in age, and height. The soldier used a cane for support, and he feigned a smile as he hobbled over to her.

"I-I thought ..." she stammered and then nodded at the soldier who promptly removed his hat. The man bore a scar from what Rose thought must be a recent wound, that ran from his left eye down his cheek. An uneasy silence passed between them.

"Are you not going to present yourself sir?"

"My apologies, permit me to introduce myself, I am second lieutenant Shaw ma'am, at your service," he said, and gave Rose a courteous bow.

"I expected to see Clifford. Do you bring news of him?"

"I do ma'am, are you his family?"

"We are acquainted, he is my ... we, are in courtship," said Rose, as she became increasingly dampened by the downpour. Shaw looked at her and then lowered his eyes to what he held in his hand before lifting his gaze to her once more.

"This will be difficult ma'am, for I bring you sad tidings indeed."

Shaw stopped talking and handed her a letter fastened with a black ribbon.

"I was in the same regiment as Mr Emberton before I was wounded. My family are not far from here and I am now discharged from the army due to my incapacity," he said, tapping his leg with his cane, "I was asked to bring this news to Mr Emberton's family. Seaforth was on the way, so I thought ..."

Shaw stopped speaking as Rose untied the ribbon that bound the letter, the back of which had been blackened with ink. She read its contents.

The message was short and forthright and not

entirely sympathetic. It told how Clifford had been found dead in his room at the hospital, suspended by the neck from a light fixture on the ceiling. No foul play was suspected, and the conclusion was that he had taken his own life. Rose could not accept as true the words she held in her hands; she read them over and over as the rain threatened to wash them off the page.

"There must be some mistake Mr Shaw, I know my Clifford would not ... would never ..."

Rose stopped talking and began to sob. Shaw did not know how he should console her in her moment of loss.

"Please ma'am, allow me to escort you to the house, the weather is—"

"Why do they think it was suicide, why?"

"Because ma'am, he was locked in his room overnight and was alone when he ... when the terrible event took place. The scuttlebutt has it that he had suffered from a fever induced madness, brought on by the guilt he carried from slaying his friend and the fear of being condemned to perish upon the scaffold. I am sorry ma'am I truly am. I should take you back inside to your family and inform them of the sad news before I make my way to the Emberton family.

"May I keep this?" Rose asked, indicating the sodden letter.

"Of course. I have a copy as is the custom."

So soon after the death of George, the news of Clifford was felt as another immense blow to the spirits of everyone at Seaforth. There would now of course be yet another funeral that the family would attend, and funerals were being planned now with ever increasing regularity. Rose and Lucille became close and were a comfort to each other as each felt their own exclusive sorrow that no other could fully appreciate. Grief had become their constant companion, a shadow forever present. Rose had cried long and hard in private as though the total power of her sadness would be enough to undo the news that had rolled off Lieutenant Shaw's rain-kissed lips and had haunted her every waking moment since.

Rose had cried long and hard in private as though the total power of her sadness would be enough to undo the news that had rolled off Lieutenant Shaw's rain-kissed lips and had haunted her every waking moment since.

She still carried the letter that Shaw had given

her, the rain thinned words inscribed upon bone-white heavy paper, its reverse side as black as a developing nightmare that reminded her of the paper Styles Hemming had used to bring his silhouettes to life. The clocks that chimed about the house with reliability could not compete with the pealing within her own mind as nothing made any sense to her now. Clifford had had so much life in him, with so much to live for, and a future that cradled them both. She was sure he would never take his own life but something did.

VI

After Clifford's burial, Lucille and Gerald had returned to their home in Blandford. Rose had taken to spending most of her days in her bedchamber, emerging only to dine with the rest of her family once in the evening but after some time her spirits had begun to recover their usual tone. Tobias had at last received a reply from Styles Hemming.

This document, as with Clifford's final letter to Rose, had been passed to me as writer of this tale by my late Uncle Cedric as an aid to further facilitate the authoring of this story. The contents have been transcribed thus:

Dear Sir,

It has troubled me to learn of your displeasure with the piece that I undertook to fashion with the upmost proficiency in my discipline. I must confess that in all my years of creating such faultless works I have not once had the slightest measure of dissatisfaction from any of my clienteles. You mentioned that an unspecified likeness had been mistakenly inserted into the scene. I can assure you sir that only the clippings that were shaped during the time of my visit to Seaforth were used to construct the picture of your illustrious family, and I am missing no other paper-works from my collections. I can emphatically confirm that only those members of the household who were present at the time of the conception of the picture were included.

Your other enquiry as to there being in some way a mechanism whereby the figures enframed are capable of movement, well sir, I declare that the knacks to which you infer, however praiseworthy of my talent, are somewhat beyond my abilities.

Pray, I hope that this account for my part helps to settle the matter for if not, I am at a loss sir as to how I am to ameliorate your grievance. Let me know at once if I can be of any further assistance.

Your servant,

Chevalier Hemming, of the Legion of Honour

"So, there you have it," said Tobias after he had finished reading Hemming's letter to his family who had seated themselves for the evening around the fire that blazed in the hearth-place.

"We are still none the wiser. Whatever the picture is doing, if indeed it is doing anything at all, it was not in its design to do so. At least, according to Hemming."

As soon as Tobias stopped talking Toddy rose from his position at Cedric's feet and became rigid, his eyes fixed upon the picture covering the chimney piece. A warning growl began to issue from the hound and no amount of effort from Cedric could pacify the dog.

The rumbles from Toddy turned into harried yaps. Rose left her chair and examined the picture; she could see at once that the scene in shadow had changed yet again. The rest of the family gathered before the picture as Rose pointed to the cut-outs of Lucille and Gerald.

"Look! The nameless one has shifted to stand betwixt Uncle Gerald and Aunt Lucille," she cried. This time there was no one who dismissed the evidence before them.

"We should warn them Papa, before it is too late," said Rose.

"Perhaps you are right," agreed Cedric, who caught the eye of his elder brother. Tobias used a bell rope to summon Hubert.

"I think it is time to rid ourselves from the

worry of this troublesome oddity," said Tobias, and impatient for Hubert to arrive, he asked Cedric to aid him in removing the heavy picture from its hook above the fire.

"What are you doing Papa?" asked Rose puzzled. Before Tobias could answer his daughter, Hubert entered the room. Tobias asked Hubert to help him stow the picture someplace where it would be out of harm's way. Rose was alarmed at the prospect.

"Oh but Papa, if we cannot see it, how are we to be forewarned?" she asked.

"We need to forget our notions about this piece. We have all become overwrought of late due to the terrible losses within the family. No, it is best for our common sense to forget we ever had the wretched thing."

Tobias was adamant that it should go and despite the continued protests from Rose, the picture was removed from the room.

"We must tell Gerald and Lucille, we simply must," said Rose to Cedric.

The cellar existed under constant shadow, there were no casements or fanlights that allowed the sun's rays to enter and to caress the castle-like cold strong grey walls. With one lantern between them, Tobias and Hubert carried the picture as they shuffled past bottle upon bottle of wine that held the sweet bouquet of long-ago summers.

They stopped when they found an empty place in which to lay the frame. Tobias covered it with some sacking plaited with webbing and thick with the dust that coheres to the grime of years.

"There, out of sight, out of mind I should think," remarked Tobias, as he rubbed the dirt from off his hands.

"*Only the darkest parts of the soul remain,*" mouthed Hubert as though only to himself and causing Tobias to ponder the meaning of his whispers. Suddenly, Hubert appeared disturbed as he turned this way and that holding out the lantern as though seeking something.

"What on earth is the matter?"

"Forgive me Your Lordship but I thought I saw —"

Hubert appeared visibly shaken.

"Hubert, I would like you to accompany me to my study if you will," bade Tobias. Hubert nodded and both men made their way up from the cool dark space below the ground.

Cedric wondered why his brother had not returned to the drawing room and so he went off in search of him only to hear both he and Hubert parleying in the study. Thinking it best to leave them to it, Cedric loitered outside where he could overhear the conversation in which both men were engaged.

Tobias poured Hubert a brandy and asked him

to sit with him so they could 'Chew the fat'.

"I think you know more than you are telling about that picture," declared Tobias, remembering how his butler almost fainted when he had first been called to identify the unknown silhouette.

"You can talk frankly with me my good man; you have known me as a boy, you have cleaned scrapes from my knees from boyish sport around the estate. You have even helped nurse me from childhood fevers. In truth, you are the most stalwart member of the household, I think of you almost as family," said Tobias warmly.

"Thank you, Your Lordship, and, if I may be so bold, I indeed look upon yourself as a man looks upon his own son," Hubert replied, who afterwards took large gulps from his brandy glass.

"Hubert, if you know something about this horrible business then now is the time to speak of it," added Tobias.

Hubert finished his drink and waited for his master to refill his glass before he began to talk.

Hubert's tale began with the construction of the most recently added wing of the house. The project was overseen by Tobias's father, the late Lord Hinchcliffe who was a superstitious soul and there were customs the old family believed in back in the day. Hubert explained how it is people's respect for the ancient ways and lore that keeps them alive. The house was built upon lands once believed to be the place of ancient spirits. In order to ensure that Seaforth suffered no ill luck in the form of fires or subsidence, a charm had to be cast, a ritual of sorts.

For the charm, a young stableboy was chosen. His name was Bran and he was the younger brother of Eve, the scullery maid who had recently been dismissed from Seaforth. The boy was brought into the main house and was told by the old lord that he was the lucky one and was chosen as a mascot for Seaforth, and he was given a 'Right royal feed-up'.

Shortly after sunrise he was taken outside where the morning dew had pearled upon the verdant lawn as the sun cast its long shadows. The boy's own shadow was then measured, and the measurements etched onto a tablet and buried, where upon the first foundation stones of the new expansion were ultimately laid. What nobody told Bran was that for the charm to be successful, the person whose shadow was used in the charm must die within the year. Hubert wanted to warn the boy but at the time he was merely the underbutler to his senior predecessor. Knowing how his time was approaching when he would step into the role of butler at Seaforth, Hubert did not want to ruin his chances of such a long-lasting career, so he kept everything to himself.

Within the year, Bran went missing and after a search was made by the chief groomsman and coachmen, he was found at the foot of the cliffs below Old Nick's Point. The boy had been fatally wounded by the fall where his body was broken beyond healing. During that time, an eerie and dense grim fog had crept in from the sea the likes of which had 'Ne'er been seen since'. Hubert likened it to a waterfall of mist in reverse rolling up over the cliffs. It was believed that Bran had lost his way in the murk and had tumbled over the cliffs, although his sister Eve, always suspected that her brother had met his end by other nefarious means.

Bran was hoisted by ropes up to the clifftop and brought back to Seaforth where he was subsequently put to bed in one of the vacant servant rooms. He lingered on the brink of death for many days; his body endured widespread gangrene and for the most part had turned black as coal. He died in excruciating agony and his manner of death had a profound effect on the old Lord Hinchcliffe whose health suffered from it up until his own demise.

Eve and the rest of the servants back in the day believed Bran's death room had become haunted since his decease. There was a sinister atmosphere about the room and all bar Eve refused to go near it. Some of the younger maids claimed to have seen shadowy forms floating through rooms where doors had been locked. Eve had heard about the ritual before the laying of the foundation stones. She did not like to think of her little brother's spirit being forever trapped within the house and she began to leave offerings of food and drink and other simple gifts. This she had confessed to during her discharge. Of one thing Eve was certain - that if the offerings used to pacify Bran's wandering spirit were taken away, then he may try to reclaim them and even act out revenge, wreaking death and destruction on those who had tricked him and trapped his soul within the dark and sombre walls of Seaforth.

The following morning the household awoke to find that fog had set in and was rolling in thick from the sea and had encased Seaforth and all its grounds in its murky shroud. The whole family commented upon the unusual nature of it, and during breakfast, Hubert remarked to Tobias how the foul gloom reminded him of the time of Bran's unfortunate accident at Old Nick's Point. As coffee was poured, they each sat in silence and watched as the swirling white curls outside stroked against the windows.

Rose was still adamant that Lucille and Gerald ought to be warned about the omen that foreshadowed them. Tobias told his daughter that no coachman would risk a drive in such dense fog, especially since the roads swept so dangerously close to the cliffs. Olivia reminded

Tobias how Gerald had said he would write to them to let them know they had arrived at home in Blandford.

"Did we receive a letter, Papa?" asked Rose.

"No, not yet. I expect that they have been busy after spending so much time at Seaforth," replied Tobias. Olivia furrowed her brows as she contemplated her brother's late communication.

"Should we be worried, I mean, what if Rose is right, about the picture?" asked Olivia.

"Come now darling, surely you do not believe in all this jingle-brained balderdash?" answered Tobias, alarmed at his wife's sudden belief in the supernatural abilities of the picture.

"I am not sure what to believe, not after everything that has happened."

"There you are Papa; Mama can see it too!" said Rose.

"I believe I do," replied Olivia.

The fog had lingered stubbornly throughout the day and early evening. Once the drapes had been drawn to hide the unappealing scene outside, Tobias took himself off to his study to write a letter to Gerald and Lucille. Rose had feigned a headache so that she could refuse her mother's requests that she played the piano but also so she could slip away to discover where her father and Hubert had hidden the picture. She loitered outside her father's study hoping that he would vacate the room. She could not think of a better place where her father would hide something; he was after all the only one who ever used the study.

Frustrated by Tobias's steadfast occupation of the room, Rose tramped away from the study, and as she turned the passage, she almost bumped into her uncle Cedric who carried a lamp.

"Goodness, Uncle you startled me!" she yelped.

Toddy appeared from behind Cedric's legs to greet her.

"It seems everyone at Seaforth is a bundle of nerves," said Cedric. "You have the same look in your eyes that Toddy has when he is on the hunt. Are you hunting?" Cedric asked her.

"Oh Uncle, I simply cannot rest until I have found that wretched picture. I have to know if it has changed again so I can take precautions in case it is I who am now threatened."

Cedric wanted to find the picture too, and he confessed to Rose that he had thought of nothing else since it was taken out of the drawing room.

"We can look for it together," he said, before Toddy growled and scampered away down the dimly lit passage. "I believe Toddy knows where it is."

Rose and Cedric followed the hound to where he had come to rest and was scratching at the cellar door.

"Of course, the perfect place to hide it," said Rose with glee.

Cedric turned the key that had been left in the lock and the cellar door opened with a rasp. Toddy skurried past them down the granite steps and into the tunnel of gloom. They quickly followed and caught up with him. He was found pawing at the sacking that covered the picture. Cedric placed the lamp down and moved Toddy out of the way so that he could remove the grubby hessian.

Rose lifted the lamp so they could study the picture, and both let out a gasp in chorus. They could see that the anomalous figure had moved with arms extended ever closer to the silhouettes of the surviving members of the family but closest to Hubert. Before either of them could speak, a voice rang out from behind them.

"Mr Hinchcliffe, and Lady Rose."

Still grasping the lamp, Rose turned to see Hubert's rotund form carrying his own lamp.

VII

"I saw the cellar door was ajar and … what are you both doing down here in the dark?" asked Hubert.

"I wanted to see the picture, I had to know if, if, oh, Hubert it has changed again, and I am duty-bound to warn you that you could be in peril!" cried Rose, and she held out the lamp so that its light revealed the menacing scene before them. Although the shadows in the cellar obscured Hubert's features, both Rose and Cedric instinctively knew that he had turned pale with fear.

Before Hubert could respond to the grim news displayed before him, Rose proclaimed that she knew what must be done in order to save them all from the picture's threat. She removed a cobwebbed wine bottle from a rack where it had sat undisturbed for decades. Using the bottle as a cudgel, she violently smashed the glass that covered the silhouettes. The harsh crunch produced by her actions sent Toddy running and yelping as he made his way back out of the cellar.

Ignoring Hubert and Cedric's warnings of

potential injury, Rose removed the shards of glass from the centre of the frame. Cedric helped using a handkerchief to safely dislodge the razor-sharp slivers. With most of the shattered glass removed, Rose reached into the frame in an attempt to detach the threatening silhouette. Try as she might, she could not seem to find anything of substance to which her fingers could seize. It was as though it was not a piece of black paper clipped by Styles Hemming's reedy fingers but rather an actual shadow, tiny, and cast from somewhere impossibly far away, an echo of somebody who once was.

Hubert held his lamp up to see what she was struggling to do. He could see her shadow cast from Cedric's lamp fall across the broken picture.

"In the old times, if people broke something and then a shadow was cast over the pieces, your soul could be harmed," he said, but Rose did not hear. Frustrated with her lack of success at removing the piece she wanted, she instead unfastened the dark likenesses of all the family and friends both alive and dead. She took hold of Cedric's lamp and one by one, she burned the cuttings by placing them into the lamp's glass chimney. Individually each produced a terrible sizzling as they burned, with the last of them cracking the glass funnel.

"There, now nothing can harm us, can it?" she said.

The fire burned brightly in an otherwise empty drawing room occupied solely by Cedric. The family were all dispersed, preferring to lock themselves away in their own bedchambers. Each one appeared nervous since Cedric and Rose had returned from the cellar but it was Hubert who appeared to suffer from the most anxiety. He had brought Cedric his port and the man could barely pour it without spilling the crimson wine about the floor. Hubert nervously looked this way and that wherever he stood as though something had forever caught his eye. When he was granted his request to retire for the night, he seemed relieved and swiftly departed for his rooms as though chased by spectral imaginings all of his own.

***

Another morning and Seaforth remained cocooned by fog, and it seemed heavier, almost solid as though white paint had been applied to all the windows. When Hubert failed to appear during breakfast and after multiple pulls of the bell rope, Tobias went off in search of his butler only to find him quite dead in his quarters. Family and servants were ushered away from the grim scene, only Cedric was allowed to access the rooms.

Hubert was slumped in his chair; the window was open and fog was curling inwards only to have its misty fingers evaporate in the room. A murder of crows had perched themselves upon Hubert's chest to feast from his dead corpse. There was a sign that there had been a struggle as furnishings were upturned, papers strewn about the desk, and decanted wine was spilling over the planked floor and draining through the crevices. With Tobias and Cedric in the room, the wild birds became panicky and flapped about the space before fleeing through the gaping casement, the last of them carrying a portion of Hubert's tongue in its bill.

Neither Tobias nor Cedric could think of how to react, or what to say to one another. All they could do was stare in incredulity at the body of a man they had both known all their lives. What terrors he must have faced whilst alone in his room thought Cedric.

"My God, *how* he must have died," Tobias finally uttered.

Hubert's rooms remained locked. The whole household were in shock, and many complained of being able to see shadows flitting here and there about the house; there was such a feeling of fear about the place. Rose had persuaded her mother that they should vacate Seaforth without delay and they formed a formidable duo to grind down Tobias's objections to travelling in such risky weather conditions.

"If we stay here for one more day, we shall all be dead anyway Papa!" argued Rose.

"Tobias, I say we take the coach to Blandford and stay with Gerry and Lucille, just until we fathom out what the devil is going on," suggested Cedric.

"That is a most sensible idea, for my brother would not turn us away and would be glad of the company after everything that has come about of late," said Olivia.

"Right, I shall try and persuade our driver to take us, will that satisfy you?" snapped Tobias.

"Absolutely. Come ladies, we should pack with haste."

The coachman was unhappy with the idea of traversing the snaking paths that bordered the clifftops, arguing that the fog was so thick it would be reckless to attempt such a deed. In spite of his protests, he was given his orders to bring the coach round to the house as soon as he could. The family were all packed and stood upon the driveway, luggage in hand or at their feet; valets and maids too, happy to be travelling with their respective master and mistress, relieved to escape the feeling of death that had swelled within the house.

Patiently they waited as the coach made its way up to them. It was the second time that Rose thought how everything now looked like a picture created by Hemming. The grey haze had removed all the colour from the world leaving the trees, the coach, and even themselves as silhouettes against the blanket of fog. The coach came to a stop but the driver did not dismount. He remained up top wrapped in his heavy coat with shoulder cape, and his brimmed hat pulled low obscuring his face. The men loaded the luggage securing it to the back of the coach and then everyone climbed on board.

Tobias urged the driver to depart. The remaining servants stood near the entrance to Seaforth and looked on with envy as the coach set off, not one of them wanting to spend another night at the house for fear of an encounter with an unearthly visitant. As the coach was swallowed up by the miasma a cry rang out sounding distant and fog muffled. The coachman appeared wheezing and coughing through the vapour.

"'Ere why didn't they wait for me to take 'em?" he said, still breathless.

Mrs Harding looked upon him with wide eyes.

"If you're not driving them, then who is?" asked the housekeeper.

VIII

Inside the coach Olivia was protesting as they were being driven so hard and they all bounced about dangerously inside.

"I say driver, we wish to arrive at my brother's house in one piece," Olivia cried.

Cedric opened the window by sliding down the upper sash and then poked his head through the gap. The fog was rushing past in wreathes. Cedric called to the driver asking him to slow down thinking how they must be so close to the precipice at Old Nick's Point. He could see the driver huddled in his seat but he froze when he saw how the reins were loose and the horses were running unrestrained. He saw that the horses now wore funerary plumes, as black as crows' wings against the bleached ether encircling them. Cedric watched as the hat of the driver was blown away revealing the absence of a head beneath. He gasped when the driver's coat followed the hat, and it became clear to him that nobody had ever been driving them.

The horses galloped down the 'Landless Road' in what felt like a frenzy. In an instant Cedric made the choice that he would climb out of the coach to reach the reins and steer them all to safety. Ignoring his family's calls of protest, he unfastened the door but at the very moment when he was half out of the coach, a violent jolt of the carriage made him lose his grip and he fell and rolled until his body became entangled in undergrowth. Still conscious, Cedric climbed to his feet, his body was numb from his tumble but all in one piece. The low cloud was so dense he only knew that he was back on the road when the hardness was felt underfoot.

He could still hear the pounding hooves from the Friesians as they pulled the coach out of sight, and then the terrible screams from his family, and the high-pitched whinnies of the horses and then the awful silence that followed. Cedric hobbled until he fell face down upon the road. He crawled until he could hear the thunder of the sea as it smashed into the cliffs below. Reaching the sheer drop, he could see nothing as the fog was blinding his vision but he did not need to see to understand what must have happened. The track marks from the wheels of the coach told the story as they imprinted the last moments of the terrified family, undoubtedly locked in each other's arms as they plunged to the sea below.

Dazed by the horror of the incident, Cedric stumbled his way back to Seaforth and as he walked, he was plagued with the thought that nameless phantoms lurked within the murk ahead. The house eventually became visible to stand dark and grave within the fog. A familiar yelp rang out and Cedric was delighted and relieved to see Toddy scampering towards him. He greeted his hound, and the pair entered the house.

Cedric watched as the hat of the driver was blown away revealing the absence of a head beneath. He gasped when the driver's coat followed the hat, and it became clear to him that nobody had ever been driving them.

In the days that followed it became clear that Cedric's family had indeed lost their lives as he had deduced. Once the fog had diminished no search of the sea or the cliffs was made as any success at recovering the bodies was deemed hopeless. News also arrived of another tragedy. Lucille and Gerald's coach had been discovered the morning after they had returned to Blandford with both of them dead inside. Each appeared as though they had been pierced by musket fire, yet no *buck and ball* were found. Their driver had fled the scene but was tracked down by the parish constables and found to be a gibbering wreck. He faced the gallows because he could offer nothing rational in his own defence and consequently became the prime suspect in their apparent murder.

For a while, fear remained at Seaforth and the intensity of that dread was such that it induced Cedric to call upon Eve where she now lived with her brother and his wife in a cottage halfway between Neyrock and Bridport. As the new Lord Hinchcliffe, Eve was happy to accept Cedric's apologies and return to Seaforth to take up her old position as scullery maid. The increase to her earnings although welcome, was not what influenced her decision. Eve returned so that she could once more pacify her long lost brother and keep all her old workfellows in service at Seaforth safe.

Postscript

Cedric and Christina (my mother) were the only members of the family to survive that extraordinary winter. My late Uncle Cedric made it clear to me that he did not wish for the memory of this uncanny episode to die with him, and this became the main reason that I penned the narrative. As close friends and family, we all knew the story of the Seaforth Silhouettes by rote, although my mother would never entertain the idea of listening to her brother recount the most terrifying time of her life. Her second husband (my father) in contrast was captivated as I hope you as the reader are similarly appealed.

Overtime the atmosphere at Seaforth lightened; my uncle's wife and their children brought a new era to the old place. No longer did time hang about the house to stagnate within it. The walls were no longer covered with the dour ancestral portraits as they once were, with the sternest visage now worn only by the living when seated to hear my uncle's tale. Cedric eventually outlived Eve and he took on the mantle from her to leave the offerings to Bran especially in the Christmas season, where glasses of wine and spiced pies would be left around the hearths at Seaforth.

One summer the foundations were excavated and the tablet of stone where the length of a boy's shadow had been recorded was removed and the dimensions upon it were effaced and the stone cast into the sea from Old Nick's Point.

I shall never forget the last time I visited my uncle and listened as he told his ghost story to entertain his children on a cold Christmas Eve. It was the final time he voiced his tale as sadly, not long afterwards, he was taken from the world following a short but fatal illness. As always, when he had reached the climax of his story, he would bid his children to dim the lamps and request that we all look at the shadows cast from the firelight. The grate's rusty bars contained a bright fire and the light from it threw a scene upon the wall opposite like an artwork of gothic souls. We would turn to see silhouette-like shadows of a family long gone, their last moments captured for all to behold as an echo and as a warning for all those who meddle with *dark* arts.

I went by the Druid stone
That broods in the garden white and lone,
And I stopped and looked at
the shifting shadows
That at some moments fall thereon
From the tree hard by with
a rhythmic swing,
And they shaped in my imagining
To the shade that a well-known
head and shoulders
Threw there when she was gardening.

Thomas Hardy, "The Shadow
on the Stone"

BEYOND THE DROP
OF DARKNESS

BEYOND THE DROP
OF DARKNESS
I

*R*esident Nurse wanted for a Situation in a Gentleman's country house. A smart, steady, reputable Young Woman. The person appointed must be unmarried or a widow without family, to be able to read and write, be well acquainted with nursing duties required by an elderly gentleman. A respectable salary of £45 per annum is offered along with a furnished room. The position is not without its peculiarities and is thus renumerated accordingly.

The hopeful must have long and excellent endorsements and be highly commended by her last employer. She must be found to be a valuable servant to anybody that requires her service.

Applications stating age and accompanied with

recent testimonials marked: 'Application for Resident Nurse,' to be addressed to 'R. J. Chambers, Cold Stone House, Frey Hollow, Dartmoor,' on or before 30th August next. Selected candidates will have notice to attend, and their travelling expenses will be paid.

Edith Everly folded the newspaper so that the vacancy was clearly readable and seated herself at her small mahogany bureau in her room at Odell Manor. She used her finest thick notepaper and a stylographic nib, and in her best penmanship she drafted a reply to the advert. Once completed, the letter was sealed in a sturdy envelope and as she glanced at a small silver carriage clock on her chimney piece, its round porcelain dial showed that she had already missed the last post. She tucked the envelope into the top corner of the tall pier glass mirror that hung between the two windows in her room so that she would not forget to have it posted early the next day.

Edith was twenty-four years of age and because she was yet unmarried, she earned money as a governess for a young master in order to give herself some independence. Miles, the boy in question, she thought of as a spoilt and churlish imp who was often taken by fits of temper over the smallest trifles. It was Edith thought, as though sometimes he had the very Devil in him and occasionally needed to be held down until he was placated. The rest of the household were equally bothersome to Edith, including the cook who was so incompetent at her profession, most of what she prepared was inedible and, on many occasions, Edith had accused her of 'not knowing how to cook hot water!'

Edith found her employer, Lady Elizabeth Ainsley equally as annoying as her progeny. She had the same unbalanced temperament as her son and to make matters worse, she was completely deaf and heard nothing unless one positively roared at her. It was no wonder thought Edith, that her husband worked abroad for most of the year.

Remaining in the Ainsley's employ for Edith was an endurance greater than no other, and she only tolerated it because similar positions around London were becoming hard to find due to a recent downturn in the wealth of the once opulent houses. Her own family lived a satisfactory life. Her father being a parson, meant Edith's childhood had been a comfortable one living in a charming rectory, which she adored and only left when the position at the Ainsleys' presented itself. Determined to find a way out of her present unsatisfactory station she set upon the plan of finding alternative employment with the greatest ardour.

When she saw the advert in the 'London Gazette', she could not believe the salary being offered as it was double her current earnings. She had no experience of nursing an elderly gentleman only children but she was certain it could in no way be as difficult and as thorny a task as her present engagement. Although never one to perjure herself, and especially due to being the daughter of a clergyman, she saw on this occasion no harm in stretching the truth and she had written in her application that she had once been a nursemaid to her 'ailing father' even though of course he was of sound health. He had though once suffered from a fever which almost took him from the bosom of the family so she believed that she was in fact merely elaborating the story and it was a necessary act due to the probability of an unremarkable reference she would undoubtably receive from Lady Ainsley if she were to hand in her notice.

The next morning, she posted her reply to the advert and heard nothing more for four whole weeks and had given up hope until the sixth of September when a letter was handed to her that morning as she was preparing one of Miles' daily lessons. The note was penned upon fine paper with an embossed border and contained the family crest of Mr R. J. Chambers:

R. J. Chambers,

Cold Stone House, Frey Hollow, Dartmoor.

Sept. 1ˢᵗ 1876

Dear Ms Edith Everly,

I formally request the pleasure of your attendance at eleven o'clock on Tuesday 4ᵗʰ October to discuss matters involving the situation of Resident Nurse. Please respond directly to either decline or accept the appointment. Travelling & accommodation expenses will be reimbursed upon arrival.

Sincerely Yours,

Roderick J Chambers

    Edith hurriedly penned a reply and asked a hall boy to deliver it to the post forthwith. Again, she felt forced to tell an untruth and concoct a tale about how her mother had become ill. Her little ruse was accepted, and she was given leave to pay a visit to her parental home but planned instead to use the time to take a train to Okehampton so she could attend her interview at Cold Stone House.

***

    The journey to Okehampton was lengthy. Edith wore her finest carriage dress and bonnet and took only two pieces of light luggage for the trip. The train rocked her gently as she sat in the coach and the grime from the engines smutted the glass but it could not conceal the beauty of the countryside as it rolled by the windows. The greens of the terrain reflected brightly under the sun burning in a blue sky, made even more pretty for all the scattered puffs of cloud.

It was early evening when the train pulled into Okehampton station. Edith took a hansom cab to the Candlesnuffer Inn at Frey Hollow. It was, the cabbie said, 'hospitable enough, serving a good variety of grub, and fine ale!' On arrival she paid the cabbie and watched as the horses were turned and the carriage was driven back the way they had come. She looked at the inn; it was an old stone building embracing the little winding lane from which it grew. The front was sporting a brilliant new coat that gleamed under the golden light of evening but the sides had a texture that told of its battles against the elements spanning many mortal lifetimes.

The interior of the inn was full of pastoral charm; there were slate floors, large fireplaces, and low-beamed ceilings throughout. Edith enquired about rooms and was happy to hear that there were several available for the night and all at a reasonable cost. She took the cheapest so that when reimbursed for travel and lodgings, Mr R. J. Chambers might look upon her favourably, rather than if she were to present him with a more exorbitant tab.

The remainder of the evening she spent in her room which was snug, yet sufficient for her needs, only leaving it to bring in a tray of supper that had been carried up and left outside her door. The sounds of merrymaking continued well into the midnight hour but eventually the inn fell quiet, other than the noises made by the proprietors as they cleaned up after another busy day.

There was a framed map on the wall, yellowed and faded with age and it outlined the local geography of Dartmoor. Edith dressed for sleep, unhooked the map, and carried it over to the bed. Not having brought a book with her she studied it and thought about how the moors presented an inhospitable wilderness. It was a place she would endeavour to circumvent on her way to Cold Stone House if possible. With her eyes feeling heavy she stretched and yawned then placed the map down on the bedside table and snuffed out the wick on a solitary lamp. She lay in the near darkness listening to the calls of the owls outside her window whilst waiting for passage upon the ship of dreams.

The following morning after a light breakfast Edith approached the landlord of the Candlesnuffer Inn to enquire about transport to Cold Stone House. The landlord, George, was a tall and gaunt man in his early sixties with a bald and mottled scalp and he owned a pair of intense green eyes. She asked if he knew the place.

"Aye I know the place, near Foxton Mire, you'll need a sturdy carriage and equally robust driver to get you over there," said George, and he pointed towards a man who sat huddled in a corner as he ate breakfast and drank coffee.

"Ambrose will take you but if you don't mind me asking Miss, what business have you got over at that old place?"

"I have an appointment for an interview, you see there is a situation available," Edith replied. George began wiping the counter-top with a cloth.

"Resident Nurse, is it?"

"Why yes indeed. How did you know?"

"Old Mr Chambers has had many nurses, they all stay here to begin with as you have done Miss, none of them keep their job very long."

"Oh, why is that?"

"I wouldn't know Miss but it seems, according to folk who know, Mr Chambers is very … how should I say, pernickety, if that be the word, very hard to please if you understand."

"I see," said Edith, wondering what George could be suggesting.

"Oh but don't let me discourage you especially on the morning of your appointment. You might be the one who stays, and from what I've heard, the pay is rather generous."

George pointed again over to Ambrose who

was now packing a pipe.

"Go and speak with Ambrose, he knows the way."

Edith thanked George and tentatively approached Ambrose who stopped stuffing his pipe when she was at his table.

"Pardon me but I need a carriage to take me to Cold Stone House. Would you be able to help me?" Ambrose sat silent and he appeared, as far as Edith could see, to have a grey mood matched only by the gloomy morning outside the inn windows. His voice rang out huskily into the room to ask for more coffee to accompany his eggs and toast.

"Cold Stone House," he repeated, as he looked her over. Edith nodded. Although not so old, his face nevertheless was creased and like the inn in which he sat appeared weather worn, more than likely thought Edith, from years as a driver perched above his horses.

"Come about a job 'ave you?"

"Yes, can you take me there?"

"Ambrose will take you Miss, when Ambrose has finished his breakfast," he said, referring to himself in the third person as though to exaggerate his own importance. Edith thanked him and sat herself down at a table across from him. She patiently waited for him to finish his breakfast which he seemed in no hurry to do so. When his plate and cup were finally cleared away, he looked up and was surprised that Edith had in fact waited for him.

"Suppose you'd like Ambrose to take you now," he said grudgingly. Edith nodded.

"Yes please, if it is not *too* much trouble."

Ambrose rose from his table and lit his pipe; he indicated that she should follow him, and she watched as he plodded across the room, his back arched like a wilted flower from years sat upon his carriage.

Unencumbered by luggage, Edith took with her only a leather pack which she wore about her waist. Within it she carried only a few essential items including a reticule that held a little money. The coach was decorated in yellow and black and it was not very clean on the outside, yet inside it was snug enough and there was a selection of lap blankets to choose from for the journey. Edith being the only passenger took a seat where she could face the direction of travel rather than sitting backwards. The horses she had noticed were large and powerful looking beasts, and Ambrose had remarked, before she had climbed aboard, that the *Shire Draft* horses were especially bred to be good natured as well as hardy. 'A strong horse is needed to drag a carriage across the moors.'

She was apprehensive about the journey after discovering that despite her hopes, the ride would see her taken across some of the moors to reach

Foxton Mire. Recalling how barren and desolate it appeared on the map in her room, she now could see it as it really was, and it was one of the most frightfully haunted places she had ever beheld. She settled herself in the carriage and decided to take her mind off the journey with thoughts of her approaching interview and she tried to anticipate what questions might be posed and what answers she would give to Mr R. J. Chambers. Her concentration however was constantly broken as she had to prevent herself from being tossed about within the carriage due to the wheels of the coach having to deal with the relentless rutted tracks and dips of the road.

At one point the coach stopped, and Ambrose came back to check on her due to the magnitude of the rattling. He explained that there were no roads of crushed stone like in the towns, and this made it treacherous but she should not worry as *his* carriage came with the latest steel suspensions and would see them reach their destination safe enough. The only danger being that if the rudimentary road were to become unusable because of flooding due to the recent rains, they might then have to continue off-road where there was a danger of getting stuck in a quagmire. None of these thoughts helped to cool Edith's nerves during the remainder of the journey.

Soon they turned off the moor and the eerie

open landscape was now behind them, and they were on a sturdier road. Edith saw that bare trees grew alongside the path and noticed how they appeared to be reaching upwards like skeletal hands, some bent by the wind and looking ready to grab hold of anyone foolish enough to wander close by. A house slowly emerged ahead of them which had been concealed within a heavily wooded demesne. The building was constructed entirely out of grey stone and had the form of a castellated mansion. It looked to be incredibly old and in desperate mourning for the past, being somewhat dilapidated but as they drew even closer Edith thought that it was an almost elegant decay.

The coach stopped and Ambrose was on the path and opening the door for her to step down. There was a chill to the air but the wind that had so raucously gusted as they took passage across the moors had for the time being retired. Reluctantly, Edith had to leave her lap blanket inside the carriage.

"Suppose you'll need taking back to the Candlesnuffer?" asked Ambrose.

"Yes, if it would not be too inconvenient," she said, as she paid him.

"Ambrose will be passing back later, about sundown, I 'ave to get to Portgate 'fore I get back. If you stand on the road Ambrose will pick you up, there'll be other passengers mind."

Edith thanked him and watched him climb

back aboard his carriage and drive away back towards the moors. The prospect of having to sit in the coach later, under moonlight upon the moor was altogether quite ghastly but there would at least be other travelling companions to share the journey with.

The building was constructed entirely out of grey stone and had the form of a castellated mansion. It looked to be incredibly old and in desperate mourning for the past, being somewhat dilapidated but as they drew even closer Edith thought that it was an almost elegant decay.

Edith approached the door to Cold Stone House and having found the doorbell she pulled the rope and was satisfied to hear the tinkling of a bell ringing out within. The bell retained a cheery pitch for all the solemness of the house itself. She glanced at a small pocket watch that was sewn into her dress. It was half past ten, she had made the journey in good time and was early for her appointment.

The door was opened by Arthur Farley, a tall earnest looking man wearing the livery of a butler. His hair was oiled and combed back, and he sported a long greying beard with equally silvered side whiskers. Edith introduced herself and explained why she was there. Farley stepped out from the doorway closing the door behind him. He took out a fob watch and glanced at the face.

"You are early Miss. Mr Chambers is not quite ready to see you."

Farley looked her over before speaking again.

"Have you brought any luggage with you?" he asked.

"Only this," she answered, and patted a small leather pouch she wore around her middle.

"I am afraid I have to ask if I can check the contents of your ... pack Miss," he said, pointing to the leather bundle attached to her. Edith was shocked by the sheer rudeness of the request. For any man to look through a woman's personal belongings was utterly unheard of. Farley stood resolute and insisted.

"It is the policy at Cold Stone House, and I am only acting under the authority of Mr Chambers himself Miss."

Reluctantly, Edith unbuckled the flap, removed the bag, and handed it to Farley. He glanced inside wearing an impassive expression, clearly unaffected by the broken decorum that his actions had produced. Once satisfied, he handed the bag back to Edith explaining that Mr Chambers was not a well man and for the security of his own safety, it was a necessary precaution to conduct a thorough search of her belongings or those of any other visitor to the house.

Farley stood quiet and for a moment seemed to be checking that she stood alone, at least that is what he appeared to be doing as far as Edith could tell. Pleased that all was well and good, Farley pushed open the door,

"Please come inside," he said, and Edith stepped past him into the house whilst Farley, for a moment, remained fixed upon the threshold with his eyes scanning the scene before him. Only when satisfied, he backed himself into the house and closed the door.

II

Edith followed Farley as he led her through the house. Due to the cheerless façade, she expected the interior of the house to be gloomy but was surprised to find many lamps burning brightly and they illuminated amongst other features, the historic yet dusty wall tapestries and eerily hung stuffed animal head trophies. Eventually they came to a dismal parlour, oaken panelled and filled with mysterious portraits of odd-looking people, most of which were positioned to look at one another as though engaged in furtive discourse.

"Please wait here, Mr Chambers will be with you presently," said Farley, and he gestured to one of the many chairs that seemed oddly placed about the centre of the room. Edith sat and waited. There were no windows in the room but she could hear from the chimney corner that the wind had risen again and was blowing blustery outside.

The sound of footfalls and another curious mechanical noise as something approached the room caused Edith to rise from her seat and straighten her dress. The door opened, and Farley entered pushing the elderly Roderick Chambers who was seated in an elaborate rolling chaise or Bath chair, his legs covered by a blanket and his face tight lipped and austere. Farley brought the wheeled chair to a stop. Both Chambers and Edith looked at one another; to her he was a dizzy age with sallow skin, deep set eyes, and a beaky nose. He put on a pair of spectacles that had hung around his neck on a chain and his hands rested upon the top of the wire spoked wheels of his chair as he scrutinised her.

"Have you checked her thoroughly?" Chambers asked Farley.

"I have sir,"

"Good, then you may leave us alone."

Farley nodded and left the room. An awkward silence then engulfed Edith and Chambers until he reached under his blanket and produced a piece of notepaper which Edith recognised to be her own letter of application.

"Please, sit down Miss Everly," Chambers said, and she lowered herself back into her seat. "I trust your journey was not too toilsome?"

"Not at all Sir, in fact, it was good to see some of the somewhat brooding beauty of the moor," she answered lying, for she could never think of the moor in any way other than an unsettling wilderness.

"Indeed," said Chambers, who now began to look over Edith's letter.

"It says here that you have experience of nursing your father who suffers from failing health, is this correct?"

"My father indeed was poorly but now I am happy to say is enjoying robust health!"

"I see, and no doubt, all because of your nursing proficiencies," Chambers remarked, without taking his eyes off the paper he was holding.

"That, and the grace of God Sir," Edith replied.

"I see here that you are presently employed as a governess for a young master. What is it about your current position that makes you wish to leave it to come and live all the way out here?"

Edith knew that her next answer was of paramount importance if she was ever to leave the employ of the Ainsleys, and she answered honestly but without being able to suppress the slight tremble in her voice.

"I do not draw much pleasure from my current charge as my employer and I do not always see eye to eye in spite of how hard I try, and young Master Miles of whom I have been long suffering can be so ill-mannered that he would sorely test the patience of a saint!"

Edith fell silent when she saw how Chambers was looking at her; it was a look of dissatisfaction yet with some budding mirth. Chambers enunciated the vowel 'O,' then folded Edith's letter. As he did this her heart sank believing she had said the wrong thing and spoiled her chance of being offered the position.

"You are young, and a comely young woman," said Chambers as he leaned towards her in his Bath chair. "Your hair is dark, almost as dark as ..." he fell silent as though lost in a distant memory. "It would please me to have some charm about the place. As you have no doubt noticed, Cold Stone House is appropriately named and rather devoid of any aesthetic delights."

With knobbly hands he gripped the wheels of his chair and propelled himself towards where Edith sat. He stopped inches from her, and he reached under his lap blanket and produced a small book. He handed the book to Edith who politely took it from him. It was a poetry book of works by Keats. Chambers asked Edith to read aloud a passage he had selected using the ribbon bookmark. Edith began to read 'Ode to a Nightingale' and Chambers sat back in his chair and closed his eyes and listened with intensity until Edith had finished. She handed the book back to him and he took it and nodded as the book vanished once more into the folds of his blanket.

"You have a beautiful reading voice Miss Everly, yes very agreeable," he said, and she thanked him for the complement.

"As you can see, I am an invalid, and I am limited to the confines of indoor environments."

"Surely Sir your chair is suitable for outdoor use, I have seen oth—"

"I never go outside Miss Everly, not ever!"

Chambers said, curbing her words. "Your duties will be mostly, although not limited to, looking after my needs which are not so many. I require daily medication that needs preparing and administering as my advancing age causes forgetfulness you understand. Farley and his wife have enough things to keep them occupied with having the rest of this old place to take care of."

Chambers turned his chair around and wheeled himself over to sit at a small writing bureau. He opened a drawer, produced a small tin, and placed the tin on his lap then pushed himself back over to where Edith sat.

"The most important thing of all Miss Everly is company. I have confined myself within the walls of this house for more years than I care to imagine, with only Farley and his good lady wife for company. I would like you to read to me as my eyes are not what they were you see, just my favourite poetry and of course passages from the *Good Book*. Do you play the piano Miss Everly?" asked Chambers, who was now taking money from out of the small tin on his lap.

"I do but I fear I may not be terribly good."

"Well, you could not be any worse than my last nurse, she had a peculiar talent for making sounds that one should *never* hear come out of a piano!" scoffed Chambers, before he reimbursed Edith for her accommodation and travel expenditure. Once the sum was settled, he then offered the resident nurse position to her.

Surprised at the sudden proposition, she thanked him accepting the offer and making no attempt at hiding her delight.

"I must forewarn you however, that the post does come with its whimsies, merely eccentricities of mine and nothing you should worry about. There are some strict procedures that must be followed to the letter you see. I will accept nothing but absolute adherence to the rules Miss Everly, any straying from the practices here at Cold Stone House will unfortunately result in immediate dismissal. Do we understand each other?"

Edith agreed and again thanked Chambers and they briefly settled on a starting date after Edith explained that she needed to present the Ainsleys with a month's notice before she could take up residence at Cold Stone House.

With the moorland spread before her, Edith waited at the top of the path that led to Cold Stone House. She watched Farley as he slowly walked back towards the house now partially obscured by a cobweb of bare trees. She hoped that she had not missed Ambrose's coach, he did say around 'sundown,' but she had been given an extensive tour of the house by Farley when her interview with Chambers had concluded. The house was a warren with many unused rooms whose furnishings were covered by sheets to keep off the dust. She had been shown what would be her own room once she had taken up residence at the house and was pleased to find that although a little fussy, it looked comfortable and not as austere as the rest of the house.

After explaining that she would be unable to travel back to the Candlesnuffer Inn until early evening, she was invited to dine with Chambers where she found him to be quite good-humoured with plenty of amusing anecdotes of his time as a youth and she had a burning desire to know what injury or sickness had caused him to be so debilitated and chairbound but she never asked.

Stars were beginning to show as the velvet darkness unfolded. The wind was strong again and played over the moor with absolute freedom. She began to feel a little anxious as she stood all alone with the darkness wrapping her with its own black shroud. Eventually in the distance she was able to make out the golden glow from the coach lamps and soon she could hear the rumble of the timber wheels and even make out Ambrose as he sat perched on top.

The coach stopped beside her with the horses snorting and sighing. Ambrose climbed down to the path.

"Ambrose almost overlooked you Miss, it being so dark tonight," he said, as he opened the door of the carriage for her to climb inside.

It was snug inside the coach and Edith took the only vacant seat next to a young gentleman who was eager to make her acquaintance. He lifted his topper from his head as he greeted her.

"Phillip Cotterell," he said. Edith smiled and gave her name and the introductions then spilled across to an elderly married couple, the Bennetts who sat opposite.

"I say, this journey will not be so humdrum after all," said Phillip, still smiling.

It was the woman sitting beside her husband who spoke next.

"Pray, what is it that has someone so young out on such a frightful night like this, and not to mention, alone?"

Before Edith could answer, the woman's husband spoke for her.

"You were waiting at the top of the lane that runs to Cold Stone House, I take it you are another of his nurses, meaning Chambers?"

"Indeed, or at least I shall be, you see I was only offered the position this very morning."

"Take my advice dear," said the woman, "decline it. My husband and I have met so many young things like yourself, all eager to take up a post at Cold Stone House only a short time later to be cast aside and from what we have learned, without any testimonials or character reference."

Edith thought about her interview and what Chambers had said regarding the breaking of rules, whatever they might be, perhaps her predecessors were not so diligent.

The coach slowed to a standstill and Edith was

worried that an external problem had caused the pause in their journey. She thought it might be one of the quagmires that Ambrose had spoken of, but then Phillip spoke out.

"This is my stop," he said, gathering his things together. Edith glanced out of the coach window; there was nothing in sight, only the barren moorland it seemed.

"Surely, you do not aim to get out here, where will you go?" she asked, curious about the young man's intention.

"I am here to visit my family, they have a farmstead upon the moor, *Moor-folk* I suppose you would call us. I did not wish to spend the rest of *my* life here rearing sheep, so I left to work in Exeter city. However, for all of my fleeing I am still engaged in the business of wool production in a manner of speaking," he said, and added that he looked forward to the next time that he and Edith would ride together as Ambrose opened the coach door before releasing his luggage from the rear. As the coach began to pull away Edith peered out through the window and watched as the lonely form of Phillip became consumed by the night.

The conversation inside the coach returned to Cold Stone House and Mr Chambers. The woman, who had now introduced herself as Anne, told how one of Edith's predecessors said that she had become held as a virtual prisoner at the house and that Chambers himself was terrified of the outdoors as though it had become a living thing and determined to do him harm.

"Sounds like the old boy is positively raving!" said her husband. "In fact, for many years he *has* been considered almost a lunatic. The story is that he never married after suffering an accident of some sort as a young man that resulted in him being confined to a chair. Following his parents' death, he remained at the house never leaving it, only the long suffering Farleys remained with him out of loyalty because Farleys have always served the Chambers family through generations."

"I must say that I found Mr Chambers to be quite amiable once the interview was out of the way; we both dined together and I had a pleasant time," remarked Edith in Chambers' defence.

"Just be mindful of what we tell you. It is not for us to gossip about the ins and outs of what occurs at Cold Stone House, we hardly even know the man but words of caution should never be unheeded my girl, give it some thought before you make any final decisions."

Edith thanked the couple and indeed thought about what they had told her but she had already made up her mind. The prospect of remaining at the Ainsleys' was unbearable. As the coach rumbled on, she thought about how Lady Elizabeth would react to her when she returned only to hand in her notice. It was not a pleasant thought.

III

Lady Elizabeth Ainsley stood dumbstruck before Edith. At first, she did not understand what Edith was telling her until she *bellowed* her decision to leave as governess. Once she comprehended what was being said Lady Ainsley turned purple with fury.

"You have left me in an inconvenient quandary!" she spat.

Her anger raged and Edith thought it was as though she had become a pot on the heat with nobody around them brave enough to open her lid allowing the scalding vapour within to disperse.

"How shall I find a new governess for Miles at this short notice? He has grown attached to you and the upheaval will be a tremendous shock to the boy," she ranted, before turning her back and walking away. Edith was glad of the retreat.

In truth, Miles was indifferent to her leaving as any child would be towards a departing tutor, yet on her final day he scowled at her before blurting, "I hope that you die, you horrid woman, and rot on the inside," before having one of his tantrums. Lady Elizabeth informed Edith that her testimonials would be forwarded to her once they had been written. She glanced at the note which Edith had given her and scoffed when she read the name of the residence.

"Cold Stone House, what an absurd name to call one's home, well it does not sound particularly inviting. I shall never comprehend why you would choose to leave such a luxuriant place as this."

Before departing for Dartmoor, Edith decided to pay a visit to her family in Winchester. Her work at the Ainsleys had been unbroken since she took up the post and she had a feeling that her next position would have similar restrictions on her freedom. It would be nice to see them she thought, and the rectory would provide the much-needed rest and calm that she craved before leaving for Cold Stone House.

The Rectory was old, age weathered, and rustic. The house stood in an idyllic plot embraced by the trees, now bronzed by the autumn's advance. Although she had not passed through its doors for some time, the place had a way of becoming home so instantly. As she approached, she saw her brother Luke as he tended to the garden, and he dropped his fork and ran over to greet her. With his arm around her shoulder, they went inside the house with Luke calling for their parents.

The interior of the rectory was full of furnishings from previous lives that harked back to joyful days now passed by, yet still fondly remembered. As she moved about inside, she gently brushed each chair and cabinet with her fingertips remembering them fondly. Her parents hurried to see why Luke was making such a fuss and both wore beaming smiles when they saw Edith standing before them. Her mother looked smaller yet all the same, as robust as ever, and she wore the story of a life well lived upon her face. Her father with his hair of silver was, as always, wearing the apparel of a vicar.

Edith's parents congratulated her on her news and especially on her soon to be increasing wage. With her family around her she thought about how they meant the world to her, they were her blessing, and for a moment she contemplated writing to Mr Chambers, telling him she had changed her mind and would be staying put in Winchester and never leaving the grace of the rectory again.

Later that evening, after they had all enjoyed a hearty supper, her father read aloud from a book that he took from his library. The book was a compendium of facts about Dartmoor and the surrounding townships.

"In this book it says that there have always

been people living on the moor all the way back to prehistory. In fact, it has become a popular pastime to dig up old arrowheads and pots, many of which have wound up in museums up and down the country!"

"What about your museum father," said Edith, referring to her father's own cabinet of curiosities that stood in the corner of the room where they sat. "Are you still digging things up for your collection?"

"I do find the occasional oddity, mostly Roman I think but I would optimistically say that a prehistoric arrowhead or two would not go amiss!"

"Well, I certainly shall not be spending too much time on the moor Father, and especially digging for treasures. The place frightens me. It is so wild and desolate."

"Perhaps not as isolated as you think. As the book says, there have been people living on the moor for centuries. According to this, the *moor-people* live in homes built from the grey granite stone that is prevalent in the area as are most of the houses small or grand."

Edith listened to her father as he continued to remark on fascinating particulars that he could find from his book but her own thoughts were miles away as though she was standing again before the dull stone walls of what would shortly become her home on the edge of the moor.

***

The morning arrived when Edith was to travel to Frey Hollow. After she said her goodbyes to her parents, she stood outside on the path waiting for Luke, who would be accompanying her to the station to carry her luggage. She looked back at the house she knew she would miss, nestled amongst the yellow and russet trees, whilst above her a flock of doves circled and became lit as daytime stars against an overcast slate sky.

Luke appeared in the doorway a travel case in each hand but he was not wearing his usual broad smile; instead, his brow was rumpled, and his face appeared tense. Luke hoped to follow his father into the church and ever since he and Edith were children, they had shared a secret. Luke had a gift, it was a kind of second sight, a godsend he had told her, yet she was not so sure it was altogether a good thing and certainly not the sanctifying blessing as he saw it.

As they took the lane that led to the train station Luke was unusually quiet. Edith noticed how his hair had become sprinkled with grey, and thought about how as the years rolled by, he had begun to look more like their father. At one point the companiable silence was too much and Edith decided to ask Luke what was bothering him.

"I am worried about you, that is all," he said.

"What is it that concerns you?"

Edith knew what was coming, she had grown

to recognise the signs when her brother was burdened with yet another of his foresights.

"Dartmoor is so far away, and from what you told us, it is all but a wilderness!"

Edith stopped walking and Luke put down the baggage.

"There is something else, I know it. What troubles you? Tell me Luke."

Luke took her hand in his and forced himself to smile.

"Oh, you know me Edith, my silly thoughts, my dreams. It is nothing, and I do not wish to burden you with such trifles as you set off to begin your new vocation."

"If you have had one of your visions, I would certainly like to hear of it," she said, eager that he should tell her as she remembered only too well how accurate his forecasts had been in the past. There was the time he anticipated their father's illness as though Luke knew that he had to prepare in advance for it, even speaking to the local physician to obtain advice on what one must do when caring for someone so poorly. There was also the occasion when their closest neighbour had had a fall from a horse when she was pregnant, sadly losing the baby she carried. Luke had forewarned her saying that he believed the animal had developed a feral temperament but he had nothing to back up his claims and their neighbour rejected them much to her cost. Luke never just divulged his prophecies; instead, he kept them to himself and merely tried to persuade people from following up with their plans because he had already *seen* the outcome.

"Just promise me that you will be careful and that you never go walking upon the moor, especially at night," he asked of her.

"Why on earth would I want to do that?" she said, horrified at the thought. "The place is profoundly terrifying."

"I am just being silly," he said, and he removed a necklet he wore and handed it to Edith. She saw that it was his little silver crucifix pendant. "Wear this it will protect you and make me feel much better."

"I cannot take this; it is your favourite thing given to you by Father," she said, looking at the cross upon her palm.

"I want you to take it, just until you return home."

With his own hand, Luke closed Edith's, sealing the gift inside her fist.

***

The coach ride seemed even bumpier the second time she travelled to Frey Hollow, and the rain was falling heavily and slanted and it lashed against the fine glass of the carriage windows in squally bursts. Edith wondered about Ambrose who, perched up front, had to endure the gale that was blowing across the moor. She remembered again his warnings about being stuck in a mire during flooding and hoped that today would not bring her such a misfortune. She fingered the silver cross that she now wore around her neck for comfort, as the coach lurched this way and that.

Eventually, and to Edith's relief, they drew up near Cold Stone House. Edith carried with her an umbrella but she kept it closed, knowing too well how such a strong wind would make rags of it. She covered her head with a cape as Ambrose walked with her bringing her luggage all the way up to the front porch. She gave him payment for his help, and he tipped his large wide-brimmed hat in gratitude and the rain spilled off it as water pours from a spout, almost soaking her feet. Quickly she pulled the bell chain but she could not hear the tinkling within announcing her arrival due to the howling breath of the wind in her ears. She waited, gradually becoming increasingly sodden but eventually the door opened, and Arthur Farley stood peering at her.

To Edith's frustration and disbelief, Farley insisted on inspecting the contents of her luggage before it was brought inside. She watched in displeasure as he rummaged through her two carrycases; the garments and other effects were slowly becoming as damp as she was. Eventually, he stepped aside to allow her to enter the house.

Farley looked at Edith as a puddle began to form at her feet.

"I am sorry Miss but I am bound to obey the

procedures, it is the wishes of Mr Chambers," he said, as his wife Elsie came to join them.

"Oh, goodness, you are soaked through!" fussed Elsie. "I have lit a fire in your room, you can dry out there before dinner," she said, and both Elsie and Arthur Farley each took a carrycase and led her to her room.

Edith unpacked her belongings and many items of clothing she carefully hung about the room to dry using what hooks and pegs were available. The fire was demanding a fresh pan of coal and she filled a shovel and replenished the grate but it began to smoke the room slightly. She tried to open a window to allow the haze to disperse and was surprised to find the casement nailed shut. She opened her door instead and soon the room was less foggy. To seal a window with nails contradicts the very reason and value of its existence she thought. She pondered about the fastened window and was sure that the reason was simply to deter thieves. The house stood in an isolated plot and the only deterrent to burglary that the elderly Mr Chambers had were the Farleys, his long-time domestic help.

Dinner was served up at seven o'clock. When Edith came downstairs, she was astonished to find so many lamps burning upon every available surface. Even the wall sconces were lit with stout candles and to demonstrate just how much they were used, each had long beards of wax drooping beneath. Chambers seemed delighted now Edith was finally in residence at Cold Stone House. At the large glossy dining table Chambers was seated in his Bath chair at the opposite end to Edith; both sat quietly whilst Arthur and Elsie served up the supper. As they ate, Chambers asked her about her journey and if the 'diabolical' weather had posed any challenges.

"I was, I must say, a little anxious at the prospect of becoming stuck on the moor," she told him. He could see in her expression as she spoke of the moor how afraid she was of it.

"I can understand your repugnance my dear, the moor is a demi-world beyond the drop of darkness, and especially for those not accustomed to the local terrain," he said, and both fell silent as a bluster of wind cast rain to beat against the windows. As the squall lessened Chambers added, "I myself have not set eye or foot on the moor for the past forty-eight years."

Edith nodded as if to say that she understood the reason being his disability but she felt that he was about to disclose another reason yet silenced himself as Arthur returned to the table carrying a ruby-wine carafe.

Once the tableware was taken away both Chambers and Edith remained seated to drink their wine. The claret began to numb whatever nervous tensons she had carried with her on her first day as Chambers' resident nurse and boldly she remarked on the custom of having to subject her luggage to inspection before entering the house.

"It is most disconcerting for a woman to have a man rummage through her personal effects, many of which became quite damp in the process."

Chambers apologised and said that she must not blame Farley.

"He and his good wife only act on my wishes. For matters of my own personal health, nothing *unclean* must enter this house. You do understand, I am sure?" Edith nodded but remained none the wiser for this particular protocol.

"Shall we finish our drinks in the drawing room my dear?" invited Chambers, and he rang a small brass bell that was upon the table next to his glass. A moment later Arthur appeared. Edith stood and followed Chambers as he was wheeled out of the dining room.

The drawing room, like all other rooms in the house was highly illuminated. There was a perky fire in the vast inglenook and Chambers was positioned on one side of it and Edith took up the opposite wingback chair. Arthur left the claret on a table beside Edith before leaving the room. Edith and Chambers chatted away both enjoying the warmth of the fire and the assuasive effects of the wine. Chambers spoke of the times he was a boy at the house but never mentioned what misfortune befell him confining him to his wheeled chair and his ultimate self-isolation at Cold Stone House.

A Grandfather clock rang out a short melody on its bells and gongs telling out the third quarter of the hour. It had been a long day and Edith was weary. After she announced that she would like to retire, Chambers propelled himself towards a lamp table upon which he removed a notebook, and he handed it to Edith.

"This book outlines all your expected duties Miss Everly, and all of the policies that everyone who resides here *must* follow faithfully. Pay heed and memorise it to heart as it would be a great misfortune should I have to terminate our association because of any careless mistakes."

Edith thanked him politely for the book and asked if he would like her to help him to his own bedchamber.

"No, thank you, I shall remain here for a little while," he said, and he rolled himself over to one of the large window bays raising the lamps' wicks as he passed them by. As she was leaving the room Chambers called her back.

"Oh, I asked Mrs Farley to light your room thoroughly, make no attempt to extinguish the lamps until morning. Light cleanses everything you see. If you find it difficult to sleep you will find an eye mask under the pillow."

When she entered her bedchamber, Edith was

aghast at the quantity of lamps and candles blazing away. The smell from the lamps was overpowering and she instinctively attempted to open the nailed window. Foiled, she instead used her door as a vast fan to clean the air in the room. When the fumes had dispersed, she turned the key in the door leaving it in the lock before snuffing the candles and putting out all but one of the lamps. Whatever Chambers had requested she was not going to attempt to sleep amidst such a conflagration.

***

Edith arose early the next morning as she wanted to study the *rulebook* that Chambers had given her. She gave herself a full hour before breakfast to absorb each regulation; there were many and most seemed to border on the nonsensical:

There is only one door that is used to enter or leave the house. Arthur Farley retained its only key and where it is *'necessary'* for her to go outside, she should seek him out where he will then succour her in doing so. Chambers left a comment to say, *'I hope that you will be comfortable enough at the house and will feel it unnecessary to go outside if only for the most essential reasons.'*

The book continued with its singular requests and stated that no windows are free to open and should remain so, and that nothing should be brought into the house from outside without

Arthur Farley's thorough scrutiny. All personal post delivered to the house would be inspected by Farley before being handed over. Lamps must remain lit throughout the night and only extinguished if the new day were to offer more than *'insubstantial illumination.'*

Edith carried on reading the bizarre list of demands and was taken aback at the mention of a night-time curfew where all residents of the house are *requested* to remain inside until dawn. What followed this eccentric appeal was a list of scheduled routine tasks. She was asked to administer Chambers with his medication twice daily, assist with his dressing (up to a point when going any further would infringe decorum), help Chambers with the writing of his business letters ensuring they were handed to Arthur Farley in time for the post coach, and help Elsie Farley with the daily replenishment of the lamp oil and candles.

Finally, the book ran through some well-being and comfort tasks such as reading to Chambers and performing on the piano.

As Edith finished reading the extraordinary list, she began to worry about the lamps that she had put out and the candles she had snuffed the previous night. Surely, she thought, if anyone were to check on her and found oil lamp fonts still filled to the brim and candles hardly depleted, they would become suspicious, and she would run the risk of being discharged before her new job had even begun. She tipped some lamp oil into a bedpan that she hid under a chest of drawers and used a small pair of scissors she carried on her chatelaine to trim the candles. She would dispose of the evidence at the next available opportunity.

IV

The first few weeks rolled by quickly and Edith had soon settled into her role as Resident Nurse for Roderick Chambers. She became accustomed to the unconventional set of rules that all of them had to adhere to whilst at Cold Stone House (as tiresome as they were). Her work looking after Chambers over time became routine and commonplace and both Edith and Chambers struck up a good friendship. Each evening after dinner she would sit with him in the drawing room where he would recount amusing anecdotes from his childhood, telling of his boyish mischief when he had often played tricks on Harold Farley, Arthur's late father. One of his favourite stories was the time he buttered the floor before dinner was served, and 'poor old Harold went tops over bottoms whilst carrying a platter of trout!' This reminded her of Miles and she wondered if all boys started out as little rascals but at the same time she found it hard to imagine Chambers so young and sprightly.

Most evenings, however, were spent with Edith reading to Chambers from his favourite books, mostly biblical passages, poetry or works from his own collection of classical texts. Other times he would position himself in his Bath chair close to the piano as she played for him and over time, he was becoming almost fatherly towards her as the fence between employer and associate began to disassemble.

At the end of each day Chambers would remain in the drawing room refusing Edith's offer to help him to his bedchamber. Instead he would wheel himself over to his habitual position, where he would sit and stare out of the tall bay windows lit by moonbeams as they crawled through the leaded glass to brighten his face. It was as though he was looking for someone or something. One evening she plucked up the courage to ask.

Without turning from the window, he spoke out, "Have you ever wondered what it is like to be out there, within the darkness?" he asked. Edith told him that she did not ponder over such things.

"The dark is just a curtain, a vast shadow created when the sun retires for the day," she said.

"My dear Edith, the darkness is almost like a living thing, can you not feel it? A foul of gloom filled with spirits who prowl through the world seeking the ruin of souls. They are out there and watching. Watching the house," he added.

As always she quietly departed, leaving him where he sat mumbling away to himself as though in intercourse with the spirits he had spoken of.

***

Frequently Edith began to feel imprisoned inside the house. To moderate this, she had started to accompany Elsie Farley as she went outside to the kitchen garden once or twice in the week to harvest some vegetables, and to take eggs from the hens. Towards the end of Autumn, they had a crop of onions and carrots to pull but now winter had set in, there were only some leeks remaining in the beds and cabbages growing under a cold frame.

Although the sun in December only seemed able to fill the firmament with an insipid sheen, Edith still enjoyed being outside under natural light and away from the smell of the lamp-fuel that pervaded every room of the house. She began to look forward to these mornings of harvest, carrying a basket filled with green glossy leaves and lacy roots. After they gathered the crop, there followed as Edith believed, an unnecessary examination of the vegetables and in some cases, dissections outside before the food was eventually brought into the house. At last the day came when all the harvest had been picked and the chances to escape the stuffiness of the house were mostly gone.

One morning as Edith was dressing for breakfast, she saw an orange breasted bird hopping along a grey ledge sugared with frost outside her window. The robin made her think about how Christmas was fast approaching. After breakfast she asked the Farleys if they celebrated Yuletide at the house, as so far there had been no mention of it at all. They told her they did not as Chambers thought it an unnecessary event with only the three of them in residence. The thought of not keeping Christmas at home seemed such a sad thing to Edith as she could not remember a time when she had not celebrated the festival, especially with her father being a member of the clergy. The very idea was sacrilege.

One day when the soles of Edith's boots had almost worn to holes, she was granted permission from Chambers to take a coach to town so that she could procure replacements so long as she returned 'before dusk.' She waited on the edge of the moor for Ambrose's coach to take her into town, wrapped in her warmest winter clothing as the icy winds shrieked and howled around her. Iced water, white and glittering covered the moorland in its most creative way. The chilled feathered shavings were still falling, and the scant trees caught the bounty of fresh snow in their unclothed boughs.

The coach was the only thing unwhitened amidst the dazzling landscape and she watched it slowly rattle towards her. She put out her arm and Ambrose brought the horses to a stop.

"Off to town, are we?" asked Ambrose, as she

came over to the coach.

"If you are going Sir."

"Aye, Ambrose is going, although in this weather, Ambrose must only have *one oar in the water* to attempt it!"

The door to the coach was opened from within and the smiling face of Phillip Cotterell greeted her as she climbed inside. She recognised him at once.

"Good morning, Mr Cotterell," she said, recalling the time she had sat beside him after her first visit to Frey Hollow. The young man smiled.

"It pleases me to find that you remember me after all these weeks. I take it that you are now in residence at Cold Stone House and nursing the old boy Chambers?" said Phillip, as the coach rolled on.

"Indeed, and you, are you back to visit your family on the moor?"

"Why yes, that is the very reason I am here, you also recalled *this* detail from our first meeting!" he said happily.

Edith could suddenly feel a flush erupting over her; she was not in any way attempting to be a terrible coquette but it was the informality of Phillip that seemed to bring the roses out upon her cheeks and she longed to be able to control her emotions and not have people being able to read her feelings as though she had them written across her own face. Phillip thought her blushing was the opening of her heart towards him.

"I wonder, and forgive my boldness but would you care to visit my family home upon the moor?" It was nice of Phillip to ask such a thing thought Edith, and he seemed agreeable enough but she knew that Chambers' rules would not permit it. When she tried to explain this to Phillip he made no attempt to hide his outrage at the idea of her being held as a virtual prisoner at the house.

"Forgive me Edith but it is unacceptable. I have a good mind to talk to the local constable about the matter!"

"Oh, pray put this matter out of your mind! I am in no way unhappy in my work, quite the opposite, and Mr Chambers and I have grown a good friendship," pleaded Edith.

"Well, if you insist but the man sounds completely unsound. Nevertheless, I shall call at the house to pay you a visit," said Phillip, tenaciously.

Edith said that it was best that he did not, and he dismissed her concerns. However she knew only too well that should he call at the house he would be turned away with a flea in his ear by Arthur.

Ambrose stopped the coach for Philip to get off. She watched him trudge across the moorland towards a cluster of old tenement farms and as the coach pulled away, he turned and waved, and she reciprocated and wondered if he would in fact do what he proposed and call at the house.

The town, when she arrived, was a snuggle of houses and shops amid the snow-covered heaths. There were not so many people about as most had chosen to stay indoors on such a chilly day. There were however a good variety of shops to be had, some selling medicines and others household goods. She decided to buy some cotton, needles, buttons and so on although she suspected Elsie must already have a collection of items at the house but as the Farleys themselves seldom left Frey Hollow, she assumed such stocks to be lacking in variety.

The next shop she visited was a shoemaker. She sought practical yet comfortable boots but most of them seemed decorated with intricate embroidery, ribbons and tassels, or jewels and buckles.

"Little feet wearing a pair of good boots together with a buoyant step adds charm and appearance for the lady wearing them," said the seller, but all Edith wanted was a sturdy, reliable pair of boots that would enable her to manoeuvre Chambers in his chair. To the disdain of the shoe seller but nevertheless happy with her purchase, she left the shop and crossed the street to visit a fancy gentleman's retailer.

The shop was small, dark, and badly ventilated but it was made attractive using high-quality mahogany and glass fittings and chairs were placed around the shopfloor should the customer feel tired and wish to rest. Edith wanted to buy Chambers a Christmas present and there were innumerable items on display. She was attracted to a black lacquered and bronze trimmed six-sided upright cigar holder. The proprietor demonstrated that it was also a musical box playing 'La Paloma', William Tell's Tyrolienne. Edith asked the price for the enchanting object but discovered that it had already been sold and was the only one in the shop. Luckily, she was able to place an order for another that the shopkeeper said he would happily send to the house and guaranteed that it would arrive before Christmas.

Edith's toes were feeling numb inside her old boots as she stood on the icy wayside. The ones she had just bought were still in their box but she knew they would feel much snugger and she crossed the street to the Fleece Tavern that stood on the corner where she intended to switch them over. A cursory glance at a clock tower told her that Ambrose would be yet another half hour on his return from Exeter.

Inside the tavern Edith purchased a glass of lemonade. The bartender advised her not to sit in the Public Bar as it could be 'quite rowdy at times', so she was offered the Saloon where the middle class and the gentry were separated by frosted *snob* screens. Alone and seated she pulled on her new boots, and as she laced them up, she opened one of the etched glass screens slightly so that she could watch the activities of the curious *Moor-folk.*

The patrons of the Fleece Tavern were huddled in groups; some were eating meals of stew and bread, others played cards, some appeared *corned* on ale and gin and at times burst into performances of old folk songs. The solitary drinkers merely sat taking comfort from their pipes and the singing. Edith sipped her lemonade. There was a cheering feeling inside the tavern and the firelight danced upon the faces of those within it. There were few lamps about the rooms and unlike Cold Stone House, the place crawled with shadows.

A trio of men continued their melancholy song about a girl, *Molly-O.* Edith sat quietly as the snow continued to fuse to the windows darkening the place even more and she listened to the tuneful cappella sung with rich harmonies as verse came after verse:

> ‘As I walked out one fine Christmas morn,
> As the snow blew down upon me,
> Her love appeared out of the gloom
> And her shadow crossed my path.
> Dark haired Mollie-O, Mollie-O.
> She sang her message to me,
> Oh pity me, my troubled soul
> My darling's love I still do crave.
> I then hurried home across the moor

I must remain brave,
For there she waited, dark haired Mollie-O.'

Edith stood outside Cold Stone House whilst Arthur Farley examined her box of old boots and bag of sewing things. As she waited, she looked upon the house that had become her home. She thought that if all the windows were not ablaze with lamplight, the place would almost be a dark and sombre ruin. She waited patiently as Arthur peered into the tops of her old boots as though expecting to find something but what that could be she had no idea and suspected that Arthur himself had no feeling as to what he was even looking for.

That night over dinner, Chambers was not his usual self. He sat quietly as he ate, appearing slightly withdrawn. Edith thought that his manner was one of caution, as he was wary of her and he declined her offer to wheel him out of the dining room and into the drawing room, instead preferring to propel himself to an early retreat for the night. This behaviour lasted for the best part of one entire day until eventually becoming his usual self again.

V

In the days leading up to Christmas Arthur had taken ill with a stomach upset. Edith had to step in for him undertaking his regular duties, some of which she considered excessive and pointless. One morning the post arrived, and it included a large parcel. Edith knew instantly that it was the cigar box she had bought for Chambers as a Christmas present. When she opened the outer wrappings, she could see that the shopkeeper had kindly gift-wrapped it for her and tied it with a glossy ribbon and fixed to it a card from the shop offering the compliments of the season. She quickly took the parcel to her room and hid it under the bed before returning to her daily chores.

It was Christmas Eve. The lack of festive garlands or any other Yuletide symbols at the house was for Edith deeply depressing. Chambers had told her that his enduring condition prevented him from celebrating Christmas in the usual manner and that he had 'learned to live without such unnecessary trifles.' This she found sad and felt sorry for him, trying hard to imagine how lonely and cheerless each Christmas must have been. During Arthur's recent illness she had been granted temporary ownership of the sole key to the main door. It was a large, decorative, heavy key cast from iron and was kept during the night in a key cabinet inside the pantry.

Throughout this time, she regularly went outside and the freedom of being able to do this without having to justify her reason with either of the Farleys she found most satisfying. Away from the pungent lamp fumes and surrounded by the crisp air of morning, she walked upon the unspoiled quilt of snow and approached the old holly tree. Like a grand old lady, the tree had graced the garden for as long as the house had stood there. Edith looked upon the holly tree with its deep green leaves and bright gay berries. Ivy clung to the prickly tree, and it almost looked as if the tree had grown twines of emerald hearts. Using a pair of scissors she carried upon her Chatelaine, she took some clippings and tapped them to remove the snow before putting them in her basket. With her carrier now bursting with festive trimmings she returned to the warmth of the house.

Later in the evening Arthur reappeared, his condition improved. Arthur and Elsie briefly joined Edith and Chambers in the drawing room for a glass of hot, spiced, gin punch, the only Christmas time tradition ever observed at Cold Stone House. Edith played the piano choosing appropriate festive pieces performed from memory and hoped to create a feeling of the Christmas spirit whilst the final window of advent was still open.

Both Edith and Chambers remained seated by the fireside well into the late hour. She hoped that the effects of the gin punch would have tired Chambers as she wanted to decorate the chimney piece with her holly and ivy trimmings before she turned in for the night. She thought it would be a pleasant surprise for him in the morning. Chambers however took up his usual position at the window peering outward as the snow continued to sprinkle outside. She waited in her bedchamber until a clock struck midnight before venturing downstairs carrying her basket of rich verdure and berry.

She worked quietly and quickly as Chambers slept in a room on the ground floor close to the drawing room. When she had finished, she placed the wrapped cigar box on a table near the fire and stood back to admire her work. Although she would not see the others until the morning, she was aware that it was in fact Christmas Day and a rich peacefulness seemed to envelope the house, disturbed only by the ticking of the clocks and the snap of the fire. The candlelight produced a hallowed glow upon the walls as she made her way back to her room.

There was no special breakfast for Christmas morning just the usual hard-boiled eggs, toast, and dried kippers. Chambers himself seemed oblivious to the significance of the day and acted as though for him, it brought only memories of trepidation and certainly nothing to feel pleased about. As Elsie cleared away the breakfast things, Edith decided to break the oppressive silence.

"Would you allow me to take you into the drawing room, I lit a fire earlier and I have a little surprise for you!" said Edith smiling. Chambers was rendered speechless by her singular announcement. Before he could answer she was up and had taken hold of the handles of his chair. Edith drove Chambers through the house where the gloom of the night was losing a battle to survive amidst the multitude of lamps and candles and was forced only to linger in the highest corners.

Chambers remained wordless as the spectacle of the fireplace came into view festooned with Christmas greenery that framed its welcoming hot mouth of yellow dancing flame. Edith left the chair facing the hearth and she walked over to the small table that supported her gift to him. She picked up the gaily wrapped package and handed it to Chambers.

"Merry Christmas Sir!" she said, beaming cheerfully. Her smile faltered when she saw how Chambers' face became contorted with revulsion as he looked upon the bound parcel presented to him. He raised a timorous hand, his fingers lightly brushing the colourful paper and he saw the card fastened to it and read the message from the seller.

"What is this?" he asked, keeping his eyes fixed on the offering.

"A Christmas present. I do hope you like it!" said Edith, feeling more anxious by the second as Chambers' expression of horror remained unchanged.

"Was this wrapped before being brought inside the house?"

"I … I think—"

"Pray child, was this item inspected!" roared Chambers, his voice becoming unsteady.

"No Sir, you see Mr Farley was indisposed and I knew what was inside the package having purchased it myself," she replied. With one violent swipe, he knocked the parcel from Edith's hands sending it crashing upon the floor.

Chambers cried for Arthur; he was almost screeching the man's name in mortal terror, and he looked upon Edith with the utmost wrath mixed with fear.

"Mr Chambers, I do not understand, have I done something wrong?" said Edith, seeing how frightened he was, and she attempted to go to him to offer some reassurance hoping to be able to pacify him.

"You have brought death into this house, stay away from me!" he screamed, and propelled himself away from her, the wheels of his chair crushing the shattered gift on the carpet. Edith froze as Arthur and Elsie entered looking flushed as though both had hurried beyond the capacity of their advancing years. Chambers turned his chair to face them.

"You, remove it, all of it," he spat, pointing to the mess on the floor and then to the chimney piece. "Carefully," he added, as Arthur bent to retrieve the broken cigar box that was now stuttering the melody that its mechanical innards attempted to play. Chambers sat and watched breathing rapidly, wheezing like he himself was a broken instrument.

Elsie was speedily removing the holly and ivy from the mantlepiece pricking herself as she worked, and she was about to cast the wreaths into the fire until Chambers ordered that she should completely remove them from the house along with the shattered pieces of the cigar box 'without delay.' Pulling at his hair he swung his chair to face Edith who had stood silently watching the whole undertaking with creeping anxiety.

"You knew the rules, I made it clear did I not that this position was available only to those who could abide by them. You have broken them."

"Oh Sir, I only wanted to please—"

"Enough!" spat Chambers, silencing Edith as she tried to explain.

"You have brought death to Cold Stone House, you will leave forthwith and never return, do you understand, never!"

"But Sir, it is Christmas Day," pleaded Edith.

"I care not, remove yourself," he said resolutely. Chambers propelled himself through the doorway stopping briefly to point at a lamp that had run dry of oil.

"Farley, the lamp, fill it, set a light to it. It must be lit."

Edith spent the rest of the morning packing her things. She felt devastated and disappointed with herself for being so cavalier and acting so negligently with regards to following the rules of the house during Arthur's brief absence from duties. She had lost a highly salaried job but what hurt her the most was the termination of a friendship that had developed between them, where Chambers had become almost grandfatherly towards her instead of simply being her employer.

As Edith packed, Elsie came into her room and offered some words of empathy. Edith asked her if she could think of anything that she could do to make things right.

"I have already spoken with Mr Chambers on your behalf, and I told him that your breach of the rules was only made with the best intentions," she told Edith.

"What did he say?"

"I am afraid he was resolute in insisting that you must leave but not on Christmas Day. You can remain at the house until the first coaches begin running again from Frey Hollow."

Edith thanked Elsie; although still expelled she at least had a day or two remaining, and she would try to appeal with Chambers as soon as his mood lightened.

Chambers had remained locked in his bedchamber for the rest of the day. It seemed as though he had lost his mind to worry and was acting as if he regarded the house as *unclean*. As night fell, the volume of lamps and candles increased by request of Chambers himself. Edith dined alone and still hoped that Chambers would join her, she so desperately wanted his forgiveness but he had left strict instructions with the Farleys that he was to be undisturbed.

The drawing room that evening was quiet, and Edith sat alone as she continued to wonder what could have affected Chambers so badly. Once the fire had reduced to nothing more than smouldering embers, she rose from her seat and went over to the window where Chambers habitually positioned himself night after night. She peered outside looking for a clue to his burdens but found no explanation for them. The snow flurries had finally ceased and to her delight she witnessed a fox as it scampered with light soles upon the crisp snow, its soft auburn fur caught in the warm light from the window where she stood. The animal glanced at her, its eyes in shadow before it dashed away into the glooms.

During the early hours of the morning Edith awoke to the sound of a commotion. She lay in bed and listened to the panic-stricken cries coming from Chambers' room. Quickly, she got up and put on her night robe and went to see what all the fuss was about. Chambers' door was locked, and she rapped upon it several times without receiving an answer from within other than his never-ending screaming. Soon Arthur was at her side, and he produced a key from the pocket of his dressing gown and unlocked the door.

As they entered, they saw Chambers sitting up in bed. He had the bedsheets gathered up to his chin, his eyes were wild and he was pointing over towards a corner where a gentleman's toilet table stood, the shaving mirror on top reflecting his own terrified features.

"It is in here I can see it!" he cried. Both Edith and Farley looked to where Chambers indicated but saw nothing. "Pray, do not let it take me, do not let ... *her* take me!" he wailed.

"Forgive me Mr Chambers Sir, but I see nothing," uttered Arthur as he tried his best to understand his master's crisis.

"You cannot see it? Are you blind man?" rebuked Chambers.

Again, Edith and Arthur scrutinised the corner of the room without finding anything to justify their employer's alarm. Suddenly Chambers flinched.

"It moved! For pity's sake, did you not see?"

Chambers was shaking so much that he almost fell out of the bed leaning for his chair. Edith rushed to the bedside and eased him back in and then she picked up a silver chamberstick that rested on top of a Bible on his nightstand. Carefully she walked with the candle over to the dresser. Chambers looked on with his mouth agape.

"Come back child, keep away from it!" he cried.

Edith floated the candle over and around the dresser.

"I see nothing here," she said, before Chambers barked at her.

"Below! I can see its shadow nestled beneath, watching me," he gibbered.

Edith looked to Arthur who simply raised his eyebrows in a gesture of befuddlement.

"Come away child, away," Chambers implored.

Edith stooped and almost ducked under the table; the candlelight dispersed the shadows flooding the underside with its glimmer.

"They were just shadows, nothing more," said Edith.

Chambers leaned towards her from his bed. "Are you sure?"

"See for yourself," she said, now on all fours placing the candle on the floor under the table. Chambers closed his eyes and began to wheeze as he lowered himself back to a prostrate position.

"I was sure, so sure. You must think me an old fool," he said, as he wiped away the tears of fear on the back of his hand.

Edith drew a chair near his bedside. "Not at all, it was clearly I who caused you so much distress, whatever it was I did. I am deeply sorry really, I am," she said softly.

"Would Sir like a brandy?" asked Arthur.

"No, you may leave me, both of you. I will be all right," said Chambers, his voice hoarse and chesty. Edith waited for Arthur to leave the room before she picked up the Bible from the stand next to the bed.

"I shall not leave you alone," she said. "You have had a fright."

Edith began to read from the Bible and her calm voice soothed him. Once the world of dreams had come to him, she repositioned the lamps and candles in the room to purge all the shadows. She stayed with Chambers until he stirred as the light from the new day filtered through the threadlike drapes covering the window. When he opened his eyes and saw Edith sitting beside him, her face a mask of tiredness, he was touched by her act of kindness and asked her to forgive an 'old fool' and to remain at Cold Stone House as his resident nurse.

"Pray, do not let it take me, do not let … her take me!" he wailed.

After breakfast Chambers positioned himself near to the fire in the drawing room that Arthur had enlivened with a poker. He sat with his usual blanket covering his legs and wore his night robe around his shoulders. He complained about feeling a chill even though the room had been made snug enough. Edith could see that the fright Chambers had suffered during the night had lingered and she was about to fetch him a warming drink when he asked her to stay. She sat in a chair opposite him as he began to disclose the cause of his fears and why he felt he had to live out his life as a virtual prisoner at Cold Stone House.

VI

When Roderick Chambers was twenty-two years old, he became captivated for a while by the beauty and the wildness of a young woman called Demelza. She was one of the *Moor-folk* and she lived with her family on one of the many farmsteads that were scattered over the heaths and fells of Dartmoor. They became acquainted one dark and brooding morning as Chambers took a hike across the moorlands with his spaniel, as was his custom. The dog had dashed away to chase a rabbit and Chambers had strayed into dangerous mireland in pursuit of him and managed to become ensnared in a bog. As both his feet began to sink in the quagmire, he knew that he was in a dangerous dilemma.

Fortunately for Chambers, Demelza herself was out walking that morning, gathering herbs and mosses for her family's medicine chest. She helped by pulling him out of the bog, finding mirth in his quandary. Her laugh was unlike any he had ever heard before or since; to him it was akin to the clucking sound a hen makes whilst laying. Demelza acted as his guide all the way back to Cold Stone House because she knew the safe route between the mires. During the walk back, Chambers could not lift his gaze from her. She was a comely young woman with an alluring smile and inky hair as dark as midnight. As she walked, she seemed to be interlaced into the soul of the moor and not like he was, a body apart. There were threads of her essence in the heaths and the trees and the rivulets of water as though all were bound in a natural discourse. By the time they had reached the path leading to the house, Chambers was hopelessly besotted.

They met on the moor each day after, and every time both becoming more enamoured with the other. To her, Chambers was the rich boy from the manor and could offer her a world apart from sheep, and scrubbing, and cooking for her widowed father and three brothers. To him she was the forbidden fruit because he knew his father would never allow him a union with a common girl from the moorlands but he simply had to have her. They became betrothed in secret, each of them wearing a ring that the other gave.

Chambers was happy with the clandestine arrangement, if a matrimonial union was out of the question. He did not think that there was any harm in asking Demelza for advances of the union of the flesh. Demelza was wild, impulsive, and passionate. She loved Chambers beyond doubt, and there was nothing she would not give to him and he knew it and he took advantage of her undying devotion for him.

In her happiness Demelza began to talk unguarded to her friends at the market and soon word spread around Frey Hollow and eventually it travelled all the way to Cold Stone House. Chambers' father was furious with him, threatening disinheritance unless he broke off the engagement. At first, he flatly refused and even took a beating from one of Demelza's brothers who, after discovering them entwined together on the heathland, took it upon himself to defend her honour. It seemed for a time that nothing would set them apart until Chambers' father, in his wily way, presented to his son a refined and elegant young woman with good prospects and affluent means.

In due course, Chambers eventually succumbed to his father's wishes and the endearing charms of *Constance Anne Carmichael,* and he called off his and Demelza's engagement. In the end, he was more than happy to be free from the almost perpetual threats from his father and scuffles with Demelza's family. She, on the other hand was inconsolable, her heart and soul had been shattered into unamendable pieces and she became nothing but a *shadow* of what she once was. All the memories she had of him had turned her once safe and special moorland into a hell upon which she still walked. Her mind lost inside a dark cell with grief turning to wrath, became shackled to her as her constant companion.

One evening when all the household were seated around the chimney corner Demelza came to the house in one final attempt to try to change Chambers' mind and win back his love. His father and the elder Farley both attempted to remove her from the front doorstep numerous times but she was adamant she would only leave them alone once Chambers himself had spoken with her. To preserve the peace and to prevent any further embarrassment he went to her.

It soon became clear to Demelza that Chambers' heart had irrevocably turned away from her and no amount of pleading would bring him back. She stood before him and tugged the ring he had once given her off her finger. Poised as if to cast the ring into the night shadows and forever be lost she stopped and turned.

"No," she said, and she reached out and grabbed his hand. He tried to pull it back but she was strong, and she could see that he still wore the ring she had given him. It was a polished copper band engraved with a simple leaf and vine motif that had once belonged to her grandfather. She felt confused and wondered if there might still be a glimmer of hope or else why would he wear the ring she gave him?

"I was unable to remove it," he told her, his hand still gripped by hers. "It was always too small for me."

The scraps that lingered where her heart used to sit sank deep into her chest and she yanked off the copper band almost putting Chambers' finger out of joint; so much so that he let out a cry of pain. She backed away from him, holding up both rings for him to see. She became wild with a fervidness, and she cursed crying *'Gloaming,'* along with a flurry of other words that only the *Moor-folk* know. Finished with her outburst, she ran from the house sobbing and became lost to the shadows of the night.

Chambers never forgot the word she uttered with such venom. It was like a whistled tune or melody that sticks in the mind. *Glo—am—ing.* Whether waking or sleeping the term stuck with him.

One afternoon during an excursion to town, Chambers had quenched his thirst with a tankard of ale in the Fleece Tavern. As he sat and drank, he listened to a ditty that a huddle of *Moor-folk* sang. During their performance they mentioned the word *Gloaming* and when they had reached the end of their current verse Chambers approached them and bought them a round of ale and asked them what they knew about *Gloaming.*

It transpired that there was a superstition

amongst the *Moor-folk*. A large boulder that rested upon the moor since ancient times known locally as the 'Devil's Rock' was believed to hold magical energies. The early peoples and tribes of Dartmoor had deified the rock leaving offerings to the spirits they believed dwelt under it. These wraiths and shadows were believed to have the ability to transform a person from flesh and bone into spirit so that they could act out revenge upon those who had maltreated them in life with impunity from their mortal equals. From there after, they must forever remain, as does a crab or some other loathsome minibeast, under the rock. As their soul melds with the others who have preceded them, they collectively become an embodiment of all that is foul known as *'The Gloaming.'* It is said amongst those that know, all that is required is to place a possession of one who has wronged another on top of the stone and to call for the *Gloaming* spirits. If the object is found to be missing from the rock within the week, then the entreaty has been assented.

Chambers was horrified; always being a believer of things of an unearthly nature. He became increasingly convinced that the stories were true and that Demelza had taken the ring from his hand to place upon the rock. He could not imagine what terrible injury his own soul would suffer under the *Gloaming* curse, so he took a lantern and decided to go to her, to beg her to take back whatever bewitchment had been put on him. Crossing the moorland, he reached her farmhouse as the sun began to dip below the skyline. Before he had the chance to strike the door, it was opened and he was met by a family in grieving, and the way they spoke of their daughter and sister told him that she was in fact dead.

Demelza's father was the worse for drink, as were her brothers. They told him that she had not returned home after he had last seen her, when she had vanished into the glooms of the night upon leaving his house. They said they went out searching and found her shawl lying upon the surface of a mire where they believed she had drowned. They all blamed him saying he was responsible for her ruined state of mind, and they dragged him inside the house to give him a beating. Taking advantage of the inebriated state of the mournful men, he was able to keep them at bay enough so that he could make his escape away from the house and back across the moor. None of them followed him.

Her death had pricked his conscience but not overly. It was true that he had shared feelings with her but was it his fault that she loved him more than he loved her? He accepted their unavoidable ending objectively and it was made all the more satisfactory with the advent of the delightful Constance to whom he then became betrothed. As he stumbled over the heaths of the uplands, he could see what the *Moor-folk* called

'The Devil's Rock' now silhouetted on the skyline in front of a setting sun. He gingerly made his way over to the rock, remembering how he once had become trapped in a mire only to be saved by Demelza. He could not believe that she herself had become ensnared and sucked down to a soggy grave. She knew the safe path she had told him, and he believed her but in a grief-stricken state of mind, perhaps she had taken a catastrophic wrong turn.

When he reached the stalwart block, he rested briefly just as the last flush of sunlight was turning into the blue light of dusk. He noticed that there was a lantern placed at the foot of the rock, *Demelza's lantern* he assumed, and he exchanged hers for his as his candle was nearly spent and he used what was left of it to light the other's wick. He held up the lantern to view the stone and was surprised and relieved to see his copper ring glinting under the lantern's shine. He was right he thought, she *had* tried to curse him using the stone. Believing he had arrived in time to avert his own ruin he reached out to take the ring but before his fingers could seize it, the ring miraculously faded away as though it had melted into the stone itself. Horrified, Chambers stood there and raised the lantern as he searched the surface of the stone thinking, *hoping* that his eyes had played a trick on him but then he heard it, he heard her.

VII

As Chambers told his story Edith looked at his hands; there were deep imprints where his nails had dug in. He fidgeted in his chair as he continued.

"I believed I was safe, the ring was still there, I had got to the rock in time to save my soul, or so I thought. I searched for the ring that my eyes had seen vanish only moments before and then I heard that unmistakable laugh, her laugh, and a black shadow seemed to pour itself from under the stone. I stood there in the gloom of dusk as a dark shape, a *thing*, sometimes in the shape of a woman, and other times almost beast-like came at me!"

Edith watched as Chambers repositioned himself near the window and he gazed outside through ice laced glass as he carried on.

"I knew the thing that had surged from under the stone could not be any natural creature, even wolves and other such wild animals only live on the moor as distant memories but wolf or not, I became rooted to the spot out of mortal fear. I wished I had simply turned and fled instead of allowing the blackness of its fringe to engulf my feet. It felt like a thousand knife cuts had caused injury to my legs and the shock of it helped me to find the strength to move again. I ran and ran and when almost close to the house I fell because my legs would no longer carry me and when I looked down at them and saw them under the moon-beamy light they had withered."

Chambers swung his chair round to face Edith and he pulled away the blanket to reveal his wasted legs, and even though clothed above the ankles she could still see how shrivelled they looked. They were now merely thin bone swathed in cloth.

"I then heard her *squawking* and *clucking* again, and as I looked up, I saw *it* like a pool of black ink and there was a face emerging from within, a face I once knew and now past decay and bound for decomposition; teeth dulled and rotting, hair black and matted, a putrefied stench, it was a *thing* from the abyss."

Chambers tried to pour himself a brandy but his hands were trembling, and Edith helped him. After taking a sip of the warming drink he resumed.

"To my horror, I felt as though I was meat, and a subject to be consumed. I managed to pull myself the rest of the way to the house using my arms until my fingers bled, and always the decaying stench of what was behind impelled me to reach the door. I am I believe safe in this house because according to those who know, and for reasons I yet do not understand, a *Gloaming* spirit without bodily form cannot enter one's house unless brought in by another. It will attempt trickery as it can conceal itself about a person or within an object after making itself small."

Edith now thought that Chambers was suffering a great delusion, a fantasy concocted to expunge whatever had been the real reason for his infirmity. The Farleys must have known that Chambers was better off at Cold Stone House than if he were to become a Bedlamite. He was harmless enough and they would remain at the house as Farleys always had; it became obvious that this must be the real reason he needed a nurse.

"After I suffered the injury to my limbs Constance became cold towards me. She was a young woman as I then was a young man and not wanting to be burdened with an invalid husband, she broke off our engagement. I do not blame her for that."

He turned to look outside through the window again. "I see it from time to time out there, particularly around Christmas, a shadow moving around the house. It has inhuman patience and tries constantly with unyielding determination to get inside. Before I realised that I was to become a prisoner in my own home I discovered it nestled inside an old hollow tree trunk as I took air one morning. It knew I was there, and it will use anything it can in which to conceal itself once the sun comes up. It may take refuge under a rock, or in dips and hollows, anywhere. If you shine a light upon it, it will not wash away as normal shadows do, it will remain enduringly dark but it does not like the light. The light hurts it, I have seen it flinch under the shine from a lantern or from the rising sun. Do people not say that it is the morning that frightens the night?"

"What does this Gloaming want from you?" Edith asked, attempting to assess how much rationalising Chambers had given to his fears.

"What else other than to claim my soul as it obviously had taken Demelza's and countless others. It seeks to live within my body so it can go wherever it wants thriving safe from the daylight! If you cut me open it is dark inside, no light can get inside a body. I think Demelza drowned herself trying to avoid a fate of becoming one of the roaming dead, a carcass steered by an unearthly denizen."

"Can you not simply leave this place? You could set up home elsewhere, far away from Dartmoor."

"It matters not where I go for *it* would always find me in the end. I have already told you, it is very patient, so I have remained at Cold Stone House, my own soul trapped by that which seeks to take it. I have survived living off the income from the family estate; it is a moderate amount from the lease holders of many of the farmsteads I have steadily acquired over the years, all but one.

I shall die here by natural means and only then will I be freed from this curse!"

Chambers asked Edith if she believed him. "It is such a story sir but if you believe it with such conviction then who am I to doubt your word?"

Edith was of course lying to Chambers. She did not want him to feel as though he was alone in his troubles so she acted as any loyal friend would under the circumstances. She thought that he had been born with a disfigurement that over time worsened and had understandably destabilised his confidence as a man causing him to concoct such a tale, and over the years forgetting the fantasy of it and believing it to be true.

"I did not tell any of the others who nursed me before you came here because I feared they may feel it their duty to have me removed from the house and placed into Bedlam where I would no longer be safe," said Chambers, and he then sat quietly in his chair wringing his hands and muttering to himself in a voice too quiet to be heard.

**

A week after Christmas there was a caller at the house. Edith was unaware at the time and only learnt about it afterwards because the visitor had left her a note card. It had been Phillip Cotterell, the young man with whom she had shared two coach journeys. She presumed that he had remained true to his word and paid her a visit, and she could only imagine how awkward he must have felt after being turned away with a bug in his ear by Farley. She looked at the card and saw that he had added in ink below his Exeter city address, the name of his family's farmstead on Dartmoor. She remembered him telling her that his family were *Moor-folk,* and he must be on one of his regular visits to them, so she wrote him a formal yet friendly letter asking if he would indulge her by imparting knowledge he may have, concerning the whereabouts of the 'Devil's Rock' and removal of a *Gloaming* curse.

A few days later she was surprised to receive a reply. The notelet handed to her by Arthur was originally sealed with wax and ribbon and by the tone of Phillip's response she could tell he was delighted that she had written to him. In his letter he proposed that if a visit to the house was out of the question, then perhaps they could meet up on the moor. Following this suggestion and before his final letter-closing valediction he answered her request regarding the Gloaming curse:

'The only methods purportedly used to break a curse are to utter a prayer over the stone or to beg for mercy to release the one who is hexed. Either that, or to exchange something of value to get back the original item used in the curse.'

Phillip had even drawn her a crude map of

the moor showing the location of the stone from the road that snaked by Cold Stone House. He finished by asking why she wanted to know this as:

'Nobody believes in the 'Devil's Rock' curse anymore except for children, whose fathers and mothers use the story as a means of curtailing their bad behaviour.'

Edith thought that if Chambers believed there was a way to end his fear of the *Gloaming*, then he may at last regain some of the freedom he had lost through years of unnecessary self-imposed confinement. She intended to tell him what she had discovered so that his mind could be soothed, knowing there may be a path out from his imaginary terrors but first she wanted to see this rock for herself. Her own father had over the years cultivated within her an interest in historical artefacts and tales, and she might even discover a relic of her own, that one day could take pride of place in his collection of historic oddities back at the rectory.

One afternoon, when Chambers had taken himself off to his bedchamber complaining of lethargy, Edith's chores for the remainder of the day had become redundant. Knowing that none of the household ever went outside past midday, she took the door key from its cabinet and fastened it to her Chatelaine. Wrapping herself under a heavy shawl she slipped outside unnoticed.

Snow still clung to the heath but most of it had diminished due to recent rains. The walk across the moor instilled within her a feeling that it was indeed a place that held so many suggestions of the supernatural. The cold breath of the wind, the brooding skies and the scant stooping trees, lowering their branches as though in adoration of the land on which they grew. She followed the crude map that Phillip had made, and many times almost lost it to the wind's grip as it shrieked and gusted everywhere about her.

She could see an outcrop of rock layered upon a ridge like the backbones of some colossal dead monster and noticed a likeness to the drawing she carried. Mindful of the danger of the terrain on which she now stood, she kept to a natural path of broken granite as though formed from toppled gravestones.

When she reached the ridge, she could see that one boulder, smoother and bluer and partly detached from the rest seemed to use the wind as a voice to roar out its name at her. It had to be the 'Devil's Rock.' She stood before it and ran her hands over the rough skin, dappled with lichen and pitted by ages of rain. She glanced at her modest pocket watch and estimated that during the present season she had at least an hour before dusk by which time the house rules stipulated one must return. She wandered around the side of the rock to shelter from the wind that seemed now to blow in an exclusive direction and as she came to the other side, she was surprised to find that she was not alone.

Phillip Cotterell stood when he saw Edith appear from behind the rock. He had been sitting upon the earth sheltering out of the wind with his back against the stone. She placed a hand to her chest in shock at such an unexpected meeting. He removed a smouldering pipe from his mouth as he addressed her.

"Bless my soul! Edith,"

"Goodness, I did not expect … you have startled me so!" she said.

Phillip apologised and explained his presence telling Edith, that since he had posted her his reply, he had walked the moor path up to the ridge every day in the scant hope of a chance encounter with her.

"I was made to feel quite unwelcome when I called at the house. This seemed the only way I was sure to meet you. I hoped you would use my map and well, here you are!" he said cheerfully.

"Yes, here I am," she parroted.

"Well, and here is the darned rock you were so intrigued by," he said, patting it with a gloved hand. "Maybe now you will be able to explain your interest with it?"

From the other side and on higher ground she was now able to touch the top of the rock and she lay a hand upon it as she spoke about Chambers and some of what he had imparted to her.

"I know it is only a fable but I thought if I saw it, I might then understand a little more, perhaps I would even be able to help Chambers cast away his fears. I am his nurse, is it not my duty?"

"I am sure you mean well but the old boy is too long in the tooth for any great recovery of his senses. When you believe in something for so long, in the end it becomes a part of who you are," professed Phillip.

"You said that someone could help one who is blighted by the curse of the rock by exchanging something of value to recover the original item used in the spell."

Edith held up the silver cross her brother had given her that she had worn about her neck each day since.

"I only have this," she said, and removed it and placed it upon the rock.

Phillip lit a lantern he had brought with him and placed it down again to rest near the base of the stone; the land around them was beginning to grow dim.

"Your necklace would make a fine offering for any magpie's nest but nothing more," said Phillip, who reached out to retrieve it for her. Edith gripped his arm.

"Look," she cried, and she crouched near the base of the rock. Glittering under the lantern's soft light she saw a band half buried in the dirt close to the rock. She took her glove off and picked it out then held it close to examine. She saw it was a copper ring with an unbroken leaf and vine engraved pattern. She realised she was holding Chambers' ring. Silly Chambers, she thought. All those years believing in a curse when nothing of the kind was true at all.

The walk across the moor instilled within her a feeling that it was indeed a place that held so many suggestions of the supernatural.

Elated with her discovery, Edith wanted to get back to the house to show Chambers what she had found. She knew he would be angry with her for going to the stone but when he understood that his days of imprisonment were over, he would undoubtedly be thankful. Phillip walked with her up to the path that led to Cold Stone House. Dusk came sooner than expected and darkness began to embrace the heathland.

"Here," said Phillip as he handed Edith his lantern, "I shall not walk you to your door as I think it best if I remain unnoticed, at least for the time being."

She took the light. "Will you not need it? It is almost dark, and the mires!"

"It is only a short walk, and I will be careful. You can return the lantern the *next time* we meet. Good evening," he said smiling, and he tipped his hat before leaving the path to begin his walk across the moor.

Edith wore the broadest smile as she reached the house, most of the windows were as ever ablaze upon its sombre and gaunt profile. As she got to the door, she placed her lantern down. It had for some time stopped producing any illumination and she noticed that all the glass had blackened and assumed the cause to be soot from the guttering candle within. She took the door key off her Chatelaine and let herself in.

She crept past Chambers' bedchamber holding the copper ring, and placed the now useless lantern down behind a large potted Aspidistra with the intention of moving it somewhere appropriate in the morning. She tried Chambers' door and to her delight it was unlocked. She pushed it open and found him asleep in his chair snoring and snuffling loudly with an open book on his lap. She did not wish to wake him, so she sat herself at a small writing bureau and penned a brief note explaining that she had found his ring and asking his forgiveness for her disobeying the rules. She placed the ring and the note upon the pages of his open book and then tiptoed out through the door, closing it quietly behind her.

VIII

E dith woke to the sound of a cawing crow, and she opened her eyes in time to see it launch itself from the outside sill into the air upon sleek inky wings. She turned to look at the small chapter dial on the bedside clock; she had slept in by almost an hour. She rose quickly and dressed and eager to see Chambers, she went down for breakfast.

When she arrived in the breakfast room, she found Elsie clearing away Chambers' uneaten eggs and kippers. There was no sign of Chambers himself, so she asked where he was.

"He wasn't hungry and did not seem quite like himself at all!" said Elsie, sounding troubled. Edith now began to fear that he had taken her expedition to the 'Devil's Rock' quite badly, and before she could ask where Chambers had gone, Elsie continued with fussing over her master.

"I do not understand what has come over him, I had only just brought his breakfast in when he asked me for the key to the front door."

Edith turned and looked out through the window; no more explanation was necessary.

She saw Chambers huddled in his chair snug under a lap blanket whilst being bathed in the crisp morning sunshine. In that instant her worries drained away. It was obvious to her that Chambers, upon discovering her note and the ring, had finally unfettered himself from his self-imposed prison and was, for the first time in decades, enjoying his liberty.

It was a glorious morning. Branches of trees and twigs of bush sparkled under the cold bright sunlight as though each were adorned with gemstones and not just the melting frost. Mist was rising from the heathlands afar, and overhead the sun had painted the sky with amber and scarlet bands.

Chambers turned to look at Edith as she approached him; he was wearing dark tinted spectacles, so dark they completely obscured his eyes. He smiled at her in a way she had never seen him smile before and he offered an outstretched hand for her to take in his. She looked at the hand that now held her own, it felt cold and strong and she saw that he now wore the copper ring upon his bent finger. She smiled back at him but her smile turned into a grimace as his hand tightened into a painful grip.

"I could not bear to be encased in that airless house for one more instant," he said, and his voice sounded unfamiliar, higher in pitch and uttered with a strange brogue. Edith tried to release her hand from his grasp.

"Mr Chambers sir, you are hurting me, please!"

"This old body will not do, oh no, dear me no. The legs do not appear to work at all but you my dear have exactly what I need!"

Edith continued to struggle to release herself. Chambers began to chuckle but his laughter was more like squawking or *clucking* and she felt that there was something about him that was decidedly satanic. With her free hand she instinctively reached for her silver crucifix but it was absent, and her mind flitted back to the previous evening when she had placed it upon the 'Rock' in trade for Chambers' ring.

Chambers removed his shaded eyeglasses as a dark cloud veiled the sun and she looked at him, into inky black sockets where his eyes used to sit. It was as though everything within him, blood, brains, body, and soul had been replaced by darkness.

***

The boy sat impatiently in the school room at Odell Manor. He had discovered the room to be full of the greatest echoes owing to the tiled flooring, oaken panelled walls, and dark glossy doors. There were many bookshelves but little else in the room other than the tall windows topped with colourful glass allowing the sun's posy of rays to enter unhindered.

For the last two quarterly chimes of the clock Miles had remained seated, his legs swinging under a small desk. He had placed a piece of folded card under one leg of the desk to keep it steady whilst he carved his name upon its top using a small pocketknife. Today, his play had been surreptitiously cut short without him realising that his mother had it seemed, engaged another governess to tutor him and now he had to sit and wait for her to arrive at the school house and she was late. It made him angry because he had been bored to death sitting inside instead of where he wanted to be, out by the lakes catching fish in his net or hurling stones at the ducks that glided upon the water.

He stopped notching the desk when he heard the click-clack of shoes approaching the school room. The door opened and he was amazed to see the familiar form of Edith, his former tutor, along with his mother. Lady Elizabeth Ainsley smiled at her son.

"Miles, look who it is, your old governess has returned!"

Miles scowled his disapproval but said nothing.

"Miss Everly admitted she was wrong to leave our employ and well, I could not find any reason not to reinstate her. I thought I would keep it as a surprise, I know how you love surprises!" said his mother, and she hurried out of the school room closing the door leaving Edith and Miles alone.

Edith stood silently, and when her muteness had reached the point where it became uncomfortable Miles spoke.

"Well, are we not going to do lessons? Is that not what my mother pays you to do?" he said, haughtily.

Edith drifted across the floor to stand before him.

"Now where were we? Ah yes … I remember, you said you hoped I should die and rot on the inside." Miles felt awkward and slightly uneasy because it was true, he had said those words but he was perturbed because Edith was wearing unusually darkened spectacles and it made her face look odd.

"Well, why didn't you?" he said daringly.

"What a bad-mannered imp you are," she *clucked*. "Well, *she* did not die, not exactly but she is somewhat decaying in here with the rest of us."

Miles noticed how pale and dry her skin was, and when she removed her glasses he gasped and toppled off his chair onto the cold floor.

"You are young, so young and you have so much more life left to live, more life than this body has," she said, and reached out for him with a hand that seemed to be growing darker with every stroke of the clock, darker except for one finger ringed with copper.

*Curses are like young chickens,
they always come home to roost.*

Robert Southery, "The curse
of Kehama motto"

OF THINGS YET
TO COME.

OF THINGS YET TO COME.

I

Annie had made some coffee and we had planned to sit on our cabin porch and watch the sun set like we always did after a day's toil at the copper mine. Annie was the first to spot Earle as he rode his Buckskin towards our plot. At first, he was merely a tan blot against the verdant meadow but before long we could hear the steady beat of his four hoofed charge as he loped across the petal flecked pasture, soaked in the golden rays of a sinking sun.

We stood as he covered the last few paces before dropping to the ground and leaving his mount to chew on the turf. Earle ran the local coffee house and only mail drop point at Copper Hollow and we could see that he was waving a letter or such like, and drawing great excitement from it as he stepped onto the porch.

"Pardon me for disturbing you folks on such a fine evening 'n' all but I figured this letter might be something important."

Earle was small in stature, and without his Derby of which he was so attached, his hair was snow flecked and sparse on top but was compensated by thick wiry side whiskers and an impressive almost imperial moustache.

Earle tipped his hat politely at Annie who smiled back at him. She offered him a cup of coffee which he gratefully accepted.

"It has an English stamp on the front, though name and address is a bit hard to make out but since you're the only Englishman I know around Copper Hollow, I figured it just had to be for you Charlie!"

I took the letter from Earle and examined the elaborate handwriting on the cover spelling '*Charles Buryman.*' I was happy to make out that it was in fact my name and address and tore it open to read the contents.

"Is it something important Charles?" asked Annie, eager to hear the news. I could hardly believe my eyes and as I re-read the formal announcement printed upon the snow-white paper, I suffered inexplicably a pricking of the flesh and an uncontrollable shiver.

"Good Lord, are you OK Charlie? Looks like someone just put his boots all over your grave!" uttered Earle.

I composed myself from the shock of the news. "It is from the executors of a will, and it appears that I have been named as the sole beneficiary of the estate of my late Aunt Winifred Doyle."

"Who?" asked Annie, and she took the paper from my hand to read it herself.

"She was the wife of my mother's brother, and it seems as though she died with no family of her own to speak of," I explained.

"You've been left a house in England, and a little money too!" cried Annie excitedly.

"Well, if that don't take the rag off the bush," said Earle, swept away as I was by the good fortune. "I suppose you'll both be packing up your things and moving back to the *Old Country*?"

"Well, that's something I will have to discuss with my wife," I said, as Annie moved with a soulful gentleness and stood hands on hips watching the sky become ribbons of scarlet and gold as though she sensed a day would come when she would have to say goodbye to all she had ever known. I watched her standing there, her hair filled with hues from the last embers of the hearth to the first glow of daylight, a rival to nature's flame that warmed the treetops during the fall. She was all the copper in the world to me.

"What's it like in England?" she asked.

"A lot different than here."

"That doesn't tell me much."

"Well, I heard it rains a lot, or so I've been told," added Earle, before finishing off his coffee.

"It's funny Aunt Winifred should name me as the sole beneficiary," I said, thinking out loud.

"There's nothing funny about it, like the letter says, she had no family of her own," said Annie, taking Earle's cup for a refill.

"I think I recall meeting her only once when I

was just a boy, and as far as I can remember, she was a bit of an *odd stick*, and quite eccentric," I remarked.

"Well, if you folks decide to return to the *Old Country*, we'll have to throw a leaving party for you, not at Hank's saloon though, word got around that they had a little fuss there last week with all of 'em cowboys getting *roostered* up, drunk as skunks!"

Annie was the first to spot Earle as he rode his Buckskin towards our plot.

A fortnight later we decided that I alone should take a passage to England to gain measure of the assets that had been bequeathed to us, with the intention of settling in the land I vaguely recollected from my childhood. A couple of days after an enjoyable gathering at the Jefferson Hotel at Copper Hollow, Annie bade me a tearful yet silent farewell, after which I rode a train from Copper Mine Station to a port in Missouri and boarded a steamboat to St Louis. From St Louis

I took a packet ship to England, purchasing a boarding ticket using what little money we had banked from working at the mine; money I was saving with the intention of buying my own mine as had been my father's dream.

The voyage took five weeks, and I was fortunate enough to be able to pay for a cabin with linens, a washbasin, and other simple yet essential furnishings. For most of my other fellow travellers the voyage must have been near unbearable in the dark and cramp conditions they had to endure within the steerage with limited sanitation and privacy. It was almost a week before I found my *sea legs* and was able to walk steadily about the upper deck with freedom from seasickness, to meander amongst the seamen who operated the ship.

About halfway through the crossing I began to yield to boredom but worse was the anxiety that started to creep into my thoughts like acorn weevils, as I began to concoct scenarios that the ship might flounder under the relentless storms, sinking and condemning all on board to a watery grave. The imaginings were not so baseless as I had often read of such nautical catastrophes, and a fellow passenger I struck up a rapport with one evening within the dining saloon, relayed to me with great relish one such disaster of which he had been the sole survivor. I had to somehow snuff out my fervent imagination during the frequent stiff gales where a storm would ignite the sky like canon fire within the clouds.

On a rare calm morning and a day before we docked at Liverpool, I stood at the bow, the only passenger amongst the deckhands. I missed Annie terribly and longed for news of Copper Hollow and I saw in the deep blue fathomless seas her eyes, and when I looked skyward, I could see her hair in the sunlit tinted wisps of clouds suspended overhead. As I stood supported by the salt corroded railing, I thought about my childhood and recalled the long outward journey leaving England behind as we set out for life in a new world to follow my father's dream of making his fortune in the mining trade.

We had all arrived in Missouri as foolhardy speculators, or 'greenhorns', a term the local folk of Copper Hollow often referred to us by. Whilst we were initially rooming at the Jefferson Hotel, my father purchased a plot of land near Copper Hollow and hired some local men to help him build a cabin; the cabin that eventually became Annie's and my home. Using the remainder of his money, my father set up a copper mine to realise his dream but that dream eventually turned into a nightmare for all of us, a new life riddled with disappointment, bad luck, and bad health. The mine was unprofitable, barren, a dud, yet both my parents, God rest their souls, continued to toil until together they succumbed to the *lungers* disease and I was thus left as an orphan at fourteen.

I recall, following the burial of my dear departed mother (only eleven months since burying my father) at the 'bone orchard' at Clay Cross Cemetery, how I walked the three miles or so back to the cabin accompanied by the rains and winds of deepest winter and the silent howl of grief. Two days following the committal, Logan Hoyt, who owned the largest copper mine in the locale, sent his two boys over to the cabin to offer me work which I gratefully accepted, and remained working for the Logans the ten years since.

It was hard work at the Logan mine, harder than anything I had ever known previously. As I grew, I got stronger, and the work became less backbreaking. One of my co-workers who had originally taken me under his wing on my first morning had his lunch brought out to him each day by his daughter. I knew the first time I set eyes upon Annie that she was the one I would marry. At first, when I tried to strike up small conversations with her, she would just blush and scurry away but I persevered and eventually she began bringing me a piece of pie and an apple to go with whatever modest food I was able to prepare for myself. Shane, Annie's brother, who also worked at the mine would often chide me telling me to 'quit beatin' the devil around the stump and ask that girl to marry you!' Annie and I would eat our lunch under the tall pine trees where the earth was sprinkled with their wooden fruit. I kissed her for the first time under those trees and two years later and much to Shane's satisfaction, I found the courage to ask the question that we both longed to hear pour out from my lips and we were both wedded.

I figured that I owed it to my late father to realise his dream of owning a mine with the family name but after the disastrous start I had endured as a young boy, the Lord himself only knew my reasoning. Annie never complained about the hardships we suffered with having to save so much of the money I earned at the Logan mine so that one day we could purchase our own piece of Copper Hollow. I knew how much Annie wanted to start a family as I could see it in her face every once in a while, when we both went to town for some extra provisions, for whenever she spotted a young couple with a child, she would smile a gentle happy smile yet her faraway eyes always told a different story. We had to be practical, we only had enough money to put food on the table for the two of us let alone a hungry infant.

II

After landing at Liverpool, I took a train, stopping as near to Little Childwick as I could; the remaining distance was covered by coach. Now back on my native soil, I had forgotten how different the country looked compared with America. Through the windows in the train and coach I took in the rolling emerald-green quilts of the hills, the occasional wooded thickets, the moorlands touched with purple hues of heather, the medieval looking villages, and the snaking paths and hedgerows. It was a gentle landscape and very much in contrast to the immense wilderness of which, over the ensuing years, I had grown accustomed with its soaring mountainous ranges and even barren deserts.

I had written to the executors of my late aunt's will before I left Copper Hollow and as soon as I arrived in Little Childwick, clad in my 'Sunday Best', we had a meeting to sort out all the particulars. When our meeting had concluded, I found myself a little wealthier and was handed the keys to Doyle House and instructions on where it was to be found.

The house was only a short walk from the centre of town; flanked by ghostly white silver birch it stood in its own plot facing another similar dwelling as though looking at its own reflection in a vast mirror. When I reached the front door I beheld the visage, the pale stone skin of the house was contrasted with a set of dark staring windows. I let myself in and closed the door and was instantly pleased to find that I had been bequeathed not only the bricks and the mortar but the entire contents of the house.

I was aware that time had lingered and had become dormant in the place but as I tugged away the sheets that covered the furnishings it felt as though the whole home began to wake up from its sad slumber. The tables, chairs, and cabinets were of fine quality and notably different to the simple and unsophisticated furniture we had back in Copper Hollow. It was clear to see that my Aunt Winifred had had an eye for the finer things in life. I could picture Annie as she moved about the place exploring and showing her appreciation at each new discovery.

'My, this place is as fine as cream gravy,' I could almost hear her say, and then I began to search for any letters that surely must have been sent from home. I had copied the address from the legal letter and had given it to Annie before I left for England. Alas, I found no mail. Disheartened and somewhat concerned, I carried on with unpacking my travel case.

The daylight had dimmed as dusk began to encroach about the place and I was forced to light candles. Once sufficient illumination had been achieved, I approached the large bow window in the room to draw the curtains and as I did, I noticed the bare birches outside with their boughs plaited together to form a webbing that veiled the rising moon. I lit a fire to cheer the place and explored the bedrooms, seeking out what would become my own for the duration of my stay.

In one room a bed of oaken panels and four vertical 'barley twisted' carved columns greeted me. Rich velvet drapes hung from the tester rails and were tied back near to the bedhead, and a parcel sat atop the bed bound neatly with string. There was a letter addressed to me resting on top of the bundle also neatly fastened by ribbon. I fervently opened it hoping it was from Annie but saw it had instead been written by my Aunt Winifred.

It was a lengthy piece which began with a greeting and a hope that the garments within the package that had been left for me on the bed were 'adequately sized' and 'to my taste', adding that 'after years of living across the Atlantic, I would need sufficient tailoring fit for an Englishman; a well-dressed man is always better thought of than his shabbier contemporaries'. I placed the letter down and untied the large parcel releasing the clothing. I arranged the garments upon the bed before trying them on.

There was a white linen shirt with a stiff standing collar complete with a striped necktie. On top of this I put on a deep-necked silken vest. The trousers were grey striped and in contrast to the double-breasted knee length frock coat of tweed. To complete the ensemble Aunt Winifred had even gone to the trouble of finding a well-sized Derby hat with rounded crown. Everything fitted perfectly except for a pair of slightly loose black leather gloves. I stood in front of a long mirror and wondered what Annie would think about me masquerading as the quintessential English Gentleman or 'one of the railroad big bugs', as she would surely say.

During my travels across England, I had foresight enough to purchase a pie from a shop at the railway station which I had placed into my travel case for safe keeping. Now, as I ate my meal under the glimmer of candlelight, I read the remainder of the letter my aunt had written. She hoped that I would look upon her with gratitude for leaving me her complete estate, such as it was and that all she asked in return was a favour. The thing of which she asked of me was, I have to say, quite uncommon and somewhat ghoulish.

Aunt Winifred wrote about a blight upon the township of Little Childwick for over a century.

The local populace (some but not all) seemingly believed in a spirit that lived under the earth and feasted on the remains of the dead who were interred at the local churchyard. Before her death, my aunt asked for a custom-made coffin to be made that housed a contraption enabling one to view her corpse from above ground as she lay in repose, to ensure that it remained intact and unharmed. The reason for this dread of one's corpse suffering violence was, according to my aunt and the local superstition, that a person's spirit would feel the pain of each and every bite, scratch, and maul in the afterlife, whether that be heaven or hell, and be returned to walk the earth in unbearable agony.

I must say I found it hard to believe that people would even consider such *bosh.* As far as I was concerned, once you had *gone up the flume*, you never came back down. Aunt Winifred had requested that I check on her *condition* with regularity and that should anything appear to be amiss, I was to have her exhumed, and a special talisman prepared, to replace the original that *should* have been buried with her to protect her remains. My aunt had even left instructions as to the exact nature of the charm itself: '*Into a child's shoe should be placed a silver sixpence, a pinch of salt, and an acorn from a specified tree once used as a hanging tree. The shoe should then be laced tight and placed with the body before burial or re-burial'.* She finished her extraordinary message by adding that only a man or woman who is childless (as she had been) would be at risk of this provincial hex.

Before going to bed that night, I had busied myself setting all the clocks in the house using my own pocket watch (my late father's) as a reference source, after having religiously wound it each day during my voyage to England. The comforting cacophony of all the ticking helped to break the silence that sat heavy within the house. It was near midnight when I carried a lamp to the bedroom and left it near the bedside on a low wick. I slipped under the bedsheets and tried to sleep but the rain was drumming its fingers loudly against the windows, and the wind was noisy inside the chimney, so sleep was thwarted.

Unable to rest, I rummaged through the bedside drawers out of boredom and curiosity but found all bar one, to be devoid of any treasures or articles of interest. The lowest drawer contained a single item, a solitary shoe of an infant. I took it out and studied it as I pillowed my head. It had originally been a white shoe but age had yellowed it and I wondered if the other of the pair had been buried with my aunt as described in her letter. I also pondered if she had acquired the shoes principally to use as a talisman, or were they bought to be enjoyed and used as the makers intended.

The fact that it was yellowed with age meant that she had been in possession of the shoe for many years. I speculated that perhaps, as a young woman, she had been expecting a child only to go through the heartbreak of losing it in some sad way and she had kept the shoes because it had been too painful to discard them, preferring to keep them hidden out of sight instead. I recalled how once my mother, who always had an *old wives' tale* for any of life's affairs, warned the wife of one of the men who worked in my father's mine who was *in the family way* not to buy any clothing for the unborn because: 'It was bad luck to do so'. As I held the shoe under my gaze, I wondered if there was any veracity to some of these supposed truths after all.

My eyelids were becoming heavy, and I dropped the shoe. The sound it made hitting the floor at the bedside along with a timely squall outside, stirred me from my advancing slumber. As I opened my eyes, I saw that the drapes covering the window were billowing as though one of the glass panes was ajar. I was about to rise up with the intention of attending to the problem but froze when I saw a figure, half concealed within the flapping pleats of the curtains. I rubbed at my eyes and looked again hoping that all I had seen was a fragment from a half-formed dream, attempting to dispel itself from my own imaginings, yet it persisted and now had removed itself completely from the folds as it appeared to behold my prostrate form.

It was obvious that in life, the figure had been

a woman but now as it crept towards where I lay, it wore death's grim form, wrapped in a shroud with lice and worms from the grave grubbing in and out of the folds. The eyes were a gateway to its own deathly soul, and they looked upon me with coldness as though *it* suffered great trauma.

I stared in awe at the spirit's strange presence as it begged me for help, babbling words uttered from a dark gaping emptiness. I don't know why but I had the distinct feeling that it was the spirit of my late Aunt Winifred but whatever presence or *soul* this apparition had, it was hardly human anymore.

I have to confess that I had never before perceived an earthbound spirit but there were folks back at Copper Hollow who swore blind that they had seen the souls of men who had perished inside collapsed mines, lingering to haunt the entrance to a shaft during the hours between twilight and dawn. I was beside myself with fear and called out to the spirit to leave me be. I jumped up and drew the curtains around my bed creating a fabric screen between it and I. The bed curtains began to flutter and rise, I held on to them, pulling them taught to maintain the shield and all the while I could still hear the jabbering words and I continued to cry out, pleading for *her* to leave me alone. I hid myself like a frightened child beneath the coverlets, my palms sealing my ears, my whole body shaking like I had a fever. Somehow, and at some indeterminate time, I lost consciousness.

III

I was awakened by the trills of birds and the chimes of clocks in distant rooms. I opened my eyes and found I was lying uncovered upon the bed; the sheets were tangled and in disarray about me and the coverlet was at my feet. To anyone else, the scene would appear as though I had been engaged in a death struggle and then I recalled the visitation, my night of terror, it was an image graven upon my memory. Gingerly I reached to open the bedcurtains half expecting to find something gruesome waiting behind the veil. I was presented only with a dim room where a breach in the drapes that covered the solitary window formed a shaft of sunlit dust that warmed the foot of the bed. I began to wonder if I had dreamt the whole affair, a lifelike nightmare borne from the fatigue of a long journey and the character of a strange house. I happily convinced myself that this was the only rational explanation.

Once dressed in my new and fine apparel, I took a turn outside and discovered an old water well that had been sunk through to some underground stream. I drew some water, drank a little and carried the rest to the house. It was on my way back that I saw an iron box fixed to the stone wall that enclosed the plot. I examined the box and was pleased to discover that it was a mailbox. On the ring of house keys I found a small one that opened it, and I was delighted to find no less than six letters all written in Annie's hand.

I set a fire going in the grate and tore open the letters. I read each one in order of the postmark date and could hear Annie's sweet voice as my eyes rested upon each handwritten word. She spoke about the cabin and the way the trees in the fall had littered the fields with a copper blanket of crisp leaves like large sunburnt hands. I perceived more of a melancholy tone to her writing by her choice of phrases as the weeks rolled by and she always ended each letter by telling me how much she missed me and how lonely and long the nights were at the cabin. I cursed myself for putting her through this and feeling guilty and somewhat dispirited, I chose to save the most up-to-date letter for the evening.

I walked to town where I stocked up on some much-needed provisions. My foreign twang drew curious looks from other townsfolk as I paid for the goods at each store. I wondered if I would eventually lose the American brogue that I had allowed to smother my mother tongue? What of Annie, would she eventually begin to speak as if she had lived in England her whole life? I pondered on this as I paid a market girl for a posy of heathers mixed with berried sprigs of holly.

I was greeted at All Hallows churchyard by an angel statue blessed by the morning sun lighting its grey mottled skin. It was an imposing figure, and its face was not one of joy but of delicate grief and seriousness that untold love brings. I walked along the path that wound around the church reading the epitaphs on all the stones that had become a lure for all manner of lichen and moss. I wanted to find my aunt's resting place so I could place the posy I carried to thank her for her bestowment. As I walked, I pondered why graveyards always looked so 'grave', a place of austere stones all standing in regimented lines. Yes, a graveyard was a place that reminded us of the people we had lost but at the same time they were places of love, all the imprinted words of affection upon the stones bore testament to that.

I spotted a stone set at a peculiar angle under the shade of a yew tree, and I was drawn to its silent song, an invitation to uncover its secrets. The memorial carried a single name but not neatly chiselled as would be the custom. Here it was almost as though the inscription had been scrawled into the stone as one would apply a finger to wet clay. '*DOYLE, 1787-1865*' It *was* the name of my aunt and the date of death accurate from what little I knew but the stone itself had the appearance of being weathered by a century of rain, puzzling for someone who had been laid to rest only recently. Nevertheless, this appeared to be the marker I had sought, and I bent forwards to leave my spray of autumn flora such as it was.

Before the posy had left my fingers a voice rang out behind me. I turned to find a preacher, or rector as one would say in England. He wore the holy apparel associated with his vocation and from beneath a scalp, bald except for a strand or two of silver, he looked upon me with a wizened face, almost a map of wrinkles, mottled with age like the gravestones set around us.

"Pray, are you Winifred's family?" he said, using a youthful tone and not the croak of old age I would have expected.

I nodded. "Yes, she was my aunt."

"Then let me take you to where she was laid to rest—that is *not* her marker," he said, pointing to the lop-sided stone at my feet. Before I could dispute his claim that the stone bearing my aunt's name and date of passing was not her gravestone, he was walking back to the path whilst clutching a Bible to his chest and beckoning me to follow.

The rector, Gilbert, whose name I had learned during our walk, led me to a prominent and pristine memorial stone flanked by two pale marble cherubs. The perimeter of the plot was marked out by grave rails.

"This is the last resting place of your aunt sir,

and quite a remarkable one and not just due to its grandeur."

"What about the other," I asked. "Who else would carry the same name as my aunt?"

"Oh, perhaps a cruel joke. You see your late aunt was quite an austere woman, and not held in such a high regard by the children of the village who she would often scold if they crossed her path, as children do. She was not a cruel woman but life I fear had dealt her a savage blow and her nature suffered for it. Either that, or the other stone was a rejected burial plot she no longer intended to use."

I drew attention to the fact that the stone had her death date inscribed, yet he seemed almost to skirt around the issue.

"Some people around these parts believe in the old superstitions, I do not."

He pointed to a kind of funnel that sprouted from the ground near to my aunt's headstone. It looked like it was made from copper (of all things), and it had a place moulded at the top where one could comfortably rest their eyes. The Rector demonstrated this for me.

"It was her wish you see, and after a considerable donation to the funds of All Hallows, well, I could hardly refuse her," he said, and began to explain its function. I told him I was already aware of the apparatus after she had left me clear instructions to regularly inspect her corpse. I placed the posy I had brought into a graveside memorial vase left for that purpose.

"I shall leave you alone so that you can express your grief in private Mr Doyle."

"Oh, my name is Buryman, Charles Buryman," I corrected him, and it was then his eyes widened and his jaw became slack.

"Is there something wrong?" I asked.

"Well—I…no, nothing at all that can't wait for another time sir," he said, and his fingers gripped the Bible he carried more securely. I watched him walk away back towards the old church, stooped in thought and muttering to himself.

I was now totally alone as I stood by my aunt's grave, far from the living, and too near to the dead. The previous night's terror lingered upon my thoughts. I reasoned that the words I had read about the ghostly duty I was bound to undertake had played upon my senses before sleep. There was no other rational explanation, and as I stood in the gloomy churchyard where the puddles of rainwater shivered under the breath of the wind, I looked for sensible answers fearing that otherwise I may surrender to madness.

I closed my eyes and rested them upon the top of the little chimney. The wind rocked me as I slowly opened them; the initial blackness slowly eased into merely a murk. I inhaled as I caught sight of my aunt's cadaverous features. The viewing window only revealed the face of the corpse and a little of the neck. As my eyes became used to the dark, I could see that during her embalming, her eyes and lips had been sewn shut, presumably in order to prevent the development of a ghastly rictus grin as the features slowly decomposed in the grave.

Satisfied that I had seen enough to know that my aunt's remains were intact I was about to detach my eyes when I thought I saw something shift. I refocussed and suddenly it became obvious that I was seeing another pair of eyes locked onto mine, a cold stare of icy hostility boring into my soul. I stood back from the little chimney, reeling from the shock, and gasping for the cool December air. I tried to dismiss what I had seen rationally as I had with my vision the previous night but now I was not asleep in my bed but standing alert in the grey light of day. It was then the little window in the flue shook and rattled as if it were alive.

I am not embarrassed to say that I fled the churchyard faster than a minnow can swim a dipper and would like to add *to 'the safety and reassurance of my new abode,'* if only the place did not fill me with dread following the previous night's unnerving event. Towards the end of that day and with lamps lit and chimneys fired up I faced the onset of dusk with some trepidation. After a hearty supper and having prepared a makeshift bed of sorts on the floor in the family room (I could not bear the thought of sleeping alone in the bedroom again) I began to feel less anxious, and I remembered the letter from Annie saved for this evening and tore it from its wrapper.

I cannot express the joy I felt as I read her good news. Annie had revealed that she was in the family way and that we were both to become parents. I spent most of the evening writing a reply that would outshine any lengthy valentine note, detailing my joy at the news and the everlasting affection I had for my darling wife. I made it clear how our new financial circumstances would dispel any previous angst about affordability over the creation of our own little family. Before I had sealed the letter, I had already decided that I must return to Copper Hollow on the next available ship.

I would like to say that my new sleeping arrangement released me from any further ghastly visitations but it did not. She came to me again and this time she was at her ghostliest. She appeared gaunt, and skeletal but now there was evidence of mauling and mutilation upon her spirit I had not remembered from the previous time. With raised hands and surrounded by a luminous light the appalling sight uttered silent words from a slack jaw and like before I quailed and hid under my blanket until dawn.

The new day found me wearied from lack of

rest during the night. Once the morning had broken, I did not stop in the house longer than necessary. I was dressed and out and handed my letter for Annie over to the local postmaster before a visit to a tavern for breakfast. As I waited for my meal to be served, I spotted the rector of All Hallows sitting alone with his Bible whilst enjoying a pipe. I crossed the room to his table, and he invited me to join him. At once he noticed the shadows under my eyes and asked after my wellbeing. At first, I attributed my jaded appearance to the joys Annie's letter had brought to me and I told the rector that I was unable to sleep for thoughts of the wonderment growing inside my wife. However, I was unable to keep up the pretence for long and I blurted out the problems I was facing at Doyle House.

"My aunt's spirit has not found peace in the grave," I said, and then implored the rector that I should be allowed to do as she had asked and exhume her remains and rebury her along with a new talisman prepared as she had described.

"That is out of the question Mr Buryman, quite unthinkable!" he cried.

"It was my aunt's wishes," said I.

"What you are suggesting would be an affront upon the basic moral principle of allowing the dead to rest in peace."

"It is evident to me that my aunt clearly is not at peace, and we should do something to help protect her soul. Surely as a man of the cloth, you must see this to be right?"

"No, no, Mr Buryman, it would be seen as a sacrilegious act and what of the public health concerns? Diseases may be spread from the decaying corpse."

"Nobody but us need know about it," I pleaded.

"I am sorry but no. It cannot be done," said the rector resolutely.

I think then as I cradled my head in my hands, he could see how affected I was by all of the otherworldly visitations I had described. Whether he believed me or not, or simply thought that my recent long journey and even grief for a relative I barely knew had brought these disquiets upon me, I don't know but he asked me to accompany him back to the parsonage.

The rector's house was filled with a feeling of tranquillity and displayed a rich Jacobean style of dark brown oaken furnishings. There was a soothing ticking of a clock repeated about the place, and the daylight stole the rich tints from the colourful leaded windows that adorned the room in which we sat in two comfortable chairs either side of a lively fire. I had accepted a brandy from the rector, offered despite the early hour, in order to steady my nerves and the drink helped to dispel the ghostly echoes from the last two nights.

We sat and talked about my aunt of whom

I knew very little. I learned that she had been a staunch member of the parish congregation at All Hallows for many years but gradually withdrew following the loss of her baby daughter to heart failure, believed to have been caused by some inherited condition. We then talked about my intentions to move to England from across the ocean to set up home with Annie in Little Childwick. The exchanges between us had greatly lightened my mood, enough for the rector to feel less concerned about my nervous temper as he was when we first met at the tavern.

The rector set his brandy down upon a small table by the side of his chair.

"Do you have any other family in the town?" he asked.

I told him I did not, other than my late aunt, and as far as I knew I was the sole surviving member of the Buryman kinfolk.

"I wonder," he said, as he looked at me with his eyes fixed on mine but his thoughts elsewhere. "Would you allow me to show you something, at the churchyard?" he asked.

I agreed, and we both put on our coats and stepped outside one again to face the chilly open air.

I was led to an overgrown area of the cemetery where the rector pointed out a grave marker. The headstone had the name 'BURYMAN' carved into it with the same untidy scrawl as had been applied to the other stone I had at first mistaken to be my aunt's. It was half submerged in the earth giving the appearance that more of it existed below ground. The name *BURYMAN* was only half exposed but even so, legible.

"It must have been here for many years, and I only discovered it a couple of months ago whilst tending to the weeds. It was hidden beneath a knotted mat of ivy, and I must say that it has the appearance as though it grew from under it! I had to show it to you because I had never heard of another *Buryman* until we became acquainted. I thought you would like to see it."

The headstone had the name 'BURYMAN' carved into it with the same untidy scrawl as had been applied to the other stone I had at first mistaken to be my aunt's.

I crouched to examine the stone and again it had the look of great age by its mottled exterior. I traced my own finger along the name which although stamped in capitals was unusually joined up.

"I am afraid I must leave you with this discovery as one of my flock is gravely ill and my daily visits to his bedside have become necessary," said the rector, as he glanced at his fob watch.

"Of course, please do not let me detain you," I replied, without looking up from the singular slab of granite. As the rector took the path that led out of the churchyard I shivered under a fresh gust of a bitter wind and the shrill cry of circling crows.

'Looks like someone just put his boots all over your grave!' Earle's words uttered the moment I had first read the letter from my aunt's solicitor now returned to haunt my thoughts. I looked down to see that my own feet were placed on top of the singular grave.

IV

As I returned to Doyle House, I saw a cloaked figure peering into a front window. I could tell from the manner of clothing and stature, that the stranger was a woman. I wondered who she was and why she was scrutinising the house. Not deliberately yet quietly, I approached her and as I spoke out her arm jerked violently, and she spun around to face me.

"Goodness!" she almost screamed. "You gave me such a fright but there is nothing like a good scare is there?" she said breathlessly, as she lowered the hood of her cloak revealing her golden coils. She smiled at me, and I saw that she was a handsome woman, and at a guess I would say around the same age as Annie. She thrust a gloved hand in my direction.

"Cynthia Innes, we are neighbours Mr …"

"Buryman, Charles Buryman", I declared.

"You must think me awfully rude, finding me spying through your windows, only I knocked on the door several times and before leaving I just wanted to confirm that nobody was home. My husband Peter and I would like to invite you over for supper tonight, so that we can get to know each other. Unless you are otherwise engaged?"

"No, I mean thank you, I would like that very much," I replied, and was pleased that I now had a means to evade another lonely and fearsome evening in my aunt's house.

"Perfect, then shall we say eight-of-the clock Mr Buryman?" she suggested, still smiling. I agreed and thanked her for her kind invitation.

The Innes residence was a stark contrast to Doyle House in that there was that unmistakable atmosphere of a place well lived-in but not in any careworn fashion. The house was furnished opulently and with an elegant character but it had a feeling of warmth that Doyle House sadly lacked. My neighbours had two servants, a married live-in couple whose roles were loosely those of cook and butler. Until now, the thought had never crossed my mind for the need of housekeepers as our cabin in Copper Hollow was but a humble dwelling, whereas Doyle House could be measured at over four times the size and with Annie expecting, the need for domestic help was something that required consideration.

My hosts were friendly and courteous, and Peter Innes appeared close to my age and had a nonchalant easy manner about him where his wife, Cynthia, with whom I had already become acquainted, was somewhat extroverted and bouncy. We seated ourselves about the large, lustrous dining table gilded with all manner of tableware. As I regarded my hosts' attire, I found myself to be somewhat lacking in appropriate dinner clothing, wearing still the same apparel that I had found left for me at Doyle house. I apologised for my lack of etiquette explaining that the clothes I stood in were all I had other than my indigenous Sunday best from Copper Hollow.

"Please, do not worry Charles, Peter and I do not usually titivate ourselves so, we just wanted to make a good impression," reassured Cynthia, and I noticed that her attention hung on every word I uttered as though my adopted American brogue charmed her.

"It must be so interesting living in America," she professed.

"Indeed, how is life on the American frontier; is it as wild as they say?" asked Peter, as our dinner was served.

"I imagine you refer to stories of attacking tribes of Indians that seem to be so prevalent in the British dailies?" I inferred.

"Quite so," confirmed Peter.

"Well, there is not so much trouble these days from the indigenous people. Most were forced to leave and resettle in Indian territory where they seem quite happy to remain. All this took place years before my family set up home in a small mining town called Copper Hollow," I said, as we all began with our soup.

"Most of the people back home are *sound on the goose*, quite dependable and reliable types, it's the *roamers* you have to be wary of, most passing through from the old states back East. Oh, they are all *heeled* and bending elbows at the saloons until full as ticks. Those are the ones who like to kick up a row and create a disturbance. However, on the whole, it is trouble-free because we are a hard-working community and devout with it."

I spent the next few minutes talking about my late parent's misfortunes with mining and their untimely deaths from tuberculosis and how unexpected it was to receive the news that my only surviving relative had left me her full estate when she passed.

"I am so sorry to hear of your parents. It sounds like you have had a tough time of things old fellow but your fortunes have now changed for the better," said Peter, and he refiled our glasses with wine as our soup dishes were cleared away.

"None of us know what the fates have in store for us but you are right Peter, my luck has certainly changed, and I would like to share some more good news. I am happy to announce that I shall soon be plunged into fatherhood!" I said, and both my hosts congratulated me warmly and we raised fresh toasts to my forthcoming happy event.

"Peter and I have also tried for a family of our

own but so far we have not been blessed," said Cynthia gloomily. Peter reached over to hold her hand.

"We are still both young darling, our time will come, I just know it will," added Peter optimistically.

"I hope so or else the curse of Little Childwick may have us!" replied Cynthia, with a disturbingly worried tone.

"What is this curse you speak of?" I asked, and wondered if it had anything to do with the fable alluded to by my aunt, in her letter, regarding her own angst about injury beyond the grave.

"Oh, nothing Charles, just one of my wife's fancies. You see she believes in such supernatural humbug is that not so my dear?"

"Yes, I do believe. I have been fascinated in such mysterious things for all of my life. Enough that I have become engrossed in the arduous task of authoring what may one day be the definitive work on the subject."

"You are writing a book?" I said, with interest.

"Indeed I am. Sadly though I fear it will never be published as I do not feel my writing is all that good."

"Nonetheless, I would like to hear of this curse you speak of," I said, now feeling a little soused due to the effects of excellent wine and good company.

It was during the main course of our supper when Cynthia began to tell her account of the horror story that at one time had rocked the whole locality in apprehension. She spoke of an ill-omened couple who were childless. Unfortunately, their names had been lost to antiquity but in her manuscript, she referred to them as *John* and *Jane Mallory* due to the meaning of the name *Mallory* being *'ill-fated luck'*. Jane had been pronounced barren by their local physician leaving them both, and especially John, without an heir. John loved his wife deeply and in order to find a remedy to their procreational crisis he consulted a known local *warlock* (for want of a better term), a dabbler of unhallowed arts, whose established position in society was such as to prevent him from being gaoled or worse.

This warlock designated *The Magus* knew of only one method to correct what nature had rendered imperfect with Jane Mallory and this involved a gruesome undertaking. *The Magus* required the blood and fat from a *nameless* yet prolific regional murderer who had finally been caught and partially hanged and left to perish from the boughs of an ancient oak somewhere near the outskirts of the hamlet. The swinging man was not quite dead when they found him (on Christmas Eve of all nights), and he begged them to cut him down. When the man recognised *The Magus,* he realised that his own soul would soon be in jeopardy, if not already.

John was handed a knife by *The Magus* and was ordered to cut the body of the hanging man so that his life would drain from him into a pot placed beneath his elevated kicking feet. Before he finally expired, the powerless and strung wretch swore that as he was denied the grave then he would share it with whoever violated his body, and all the townsfolk and their descendants thereof who had condemned him to his fate.

When they had finished their grisly deed, the remaining parts of the corpse that were no use to them were cast into a hole that had been dug in non-consecrated ground. A week later, *The Magus* appeared at the Mallory's home carrying an effigy of a human infant that he had constructed from the body fat and gore of the hung killer. He presented it to Jane with the instruction that she was to treat it as though it were a *real* child.

Not being aware of the origins of the form she dutifully carried with her swathed in a blanket, she complied at the behest of *The Magus*. Over the weeks that followed the Mallory household became disturbed by an eerie wailing whenever the faux child was left in its cradle unattended. Both John and Jane wearied and unsettled by the goings-on, dreaded each new day but persisted in the rituals ordered by *The Magus*.

One day when holding the odious figure to her breast as she sat near the fire, Jane screamed raising John from his nap who after seeing blood ooze from his wife's breast snatched the swathed abomination from her grasp. On examining its ill-formed features, he was said to have heard it murmur and saw that it now had eyes of a sort that regarded him and a mouth still puckered from suckling and filled with needle sharp teeth. Without further deliberation he cast the repugnant form into the hearth where the flames eventually consumed it.

Some weeks later, Jane was pronounced to be *expecting* by the local physician but unfortunately the woman was said to have died in childbirth after delivering a baby so deformed that it had a *melted* appearance and was not expected to thrive. According to Cynthia, it had been the custom back then for a deceased mother to be buried with her child, and particularly in this case, due to the rumours that both mother and infant had been touched by occult powers. By being interred with the child before it finally expired, the belief was that the spirit of either would not return thereafter to seek out the other.

It had been such a sobering story. Cynthia freely admitted she had applied a writer's embellishment liberally in order to fill over the chasms left by time's passing, yet the main specifics believed to be anchored on some truths as they were known, remained untouched. With our dinner things cleared away we moved to another room with a cheering fire and a glass or two of good whisky. Cynthia asked me what I thought of her story and the effects of the liquor had loosened my tongue.

"Until I returned to England I did not truly believe in ghosts, yet the atmospheres within Doyle House have opened doors to all kinds of possibilities that I have to accept as true," said I.

"Whatever do you mean Charles? Are you trying to tell us that the house is haunted?" questioned Cynthia, with delight decorating her entire face. It was then I spoke about my late aunt whose spirit had visited me each night since stopping at the house. As I talked with such a nervous disposition, they were I think, compelled to believe me. I told of my aunt's wishes and how I felt duty-bound to meet the terms of my inheritance. It was then I asked Peter if he would consider helping me to unearth her remains and rebury her with a talisman as she had described.

Peter sat quietly for a while once I had finished my account. He lit a cigar for himself and one for me before he gave his answer.

"I think we should leave the dead to lie undisturbed my dear fellow, I would not want to embroil myself in such a heathen crime as this would undoubtedly be. Let the poor woman lie in peace."

"She is not at peace, and this is why her spirit subjects me to these alarming visitations I have described," I maintained.

"I would have to agree with my husband, there have been many prosecutions for those who dig up the corpses of the dead. Due to the competition for burial space in local cemeteries, there are unscrupulous clerics in the neighbouring parishes who have been known to take burial fees and then have bodies removed from graves, only to be dumped into local rivers to make space for new committals," added Cynthia.

"I simply have to do something. I beg of you please help me!"

My pleading failed to win over the help of my new friends, and I do not reproach them for it because on balance, they hardly knew me at all. Afterwards, as I sat in doleful silence, it was Cynthia who offered some new hope to the dire situation. She mentioned that the local gravedigger might be persuaded to help me and he could be found most days *'up the pole'* in the local tavern.

"His name is Seth and he is known to do anything for ale money," she informed me shrewdly. "You will recognise him as he is so tall and lean with an angry red nose."

Seth's description I committed to memory; he was all the help I had been offered if any at all.

Peter offered me a bed for the night that I accepted appreciatively; I had not had anything that resembled standard sleep since my voyage began across the ocean and subsequent stay at Doyle House. I was glad of the prospect of a *ghost-*

free night as I no longer wished to gaze upon the countenance of my deceased aunt, of which trials and wounds inflicted within the grave had made such a great alteration. After I had been shown to my room and then left alone, I peered out of the casement towards Doyle House now illuminated by the pallid face of the moon and I saw a hint of a shadowed form lingering at an upper window as though awaiting my eventual return.

V

I enjoyed a hearty breakfast with my neighbours before returning to the disquieting character of Doyle House, stopping there briefly only to collect the note that contained the instructions on assembling the talisman. The walk to the described area at the fringe of the village took longer than anticipated and was made all the more tedious due to a persistent light rain that was set in for the day. Of all the many oaks that cluttered the hillock, one stood broader and more pronounced than the rest and had the appearance of great age. It was only a deduction that this was in fact the tree as defined in my aunt's letter. Standing under its hefty boughs that formed a barrier between the insipid sun and I, it was not difficult to imagine the scenes so expressively described by Cynthia during her macabre account of the local legend.

I combed the earth beneath the tree for an acorn. Most had been squirreled away, yet I discovered several good specimens under the soggy leaves near to its foot. I pocketed the nuts and hiked back towards the plumes of smoke that rose steadily from the chimneys of the village.

It struck me as I entered through its weighty doors, how decidedly different the local tavern was compared to the ebullient saloons back home where folk gambled with cards or sung at pianos. In this drinking hole, men were sat huddled about round oak tables clutching pewter tankards in semidarkness. The walls were decorated with historic artefacts, mostly shields and swords and old mildewed hunting trophies that hung above the doors. The aroma of tobacco and stale ale from spillages yet to be mopped was overpowering but not so much as to completely disguise the delightful scents of roasting meats and stewing pots.

I scanned the room for Cynthia's description of the local gravedigger. It was difficult to discern anything in such a gloom, broken only here and there by the occasional lantern, yet my gaze was drawn towards a solitary figure sitting nearest to the snapping, leaping flames of a log fire. Although seated, his legs looked remarkably lengthy and with his gaunt frame and a nose rubicund in colour like a giant cherry, I knew I had found my man.

After purchasing two ales I crossed the room and was greeted with curious glances from well-knit patrons before I sat at Seth's table. He looked at me somewhat narked that I had disturbed his self-imposed seclusion but after I pushed the extra mug towards him briming with ale his disposition changed, and we bumped tankards and toasted each other's health.

"Do I know thee?" asked Seth, before he swallowed some of the ale. I simply shook my head and was about to explain my presence at his table when he wiped his mouth on the back of his hand then spoke further.

"When a stranger buys a man ale, it usually be because he wants somethin'," Seth said knowingly. "Well, do thee want somethin' of me mister?"

"I need your help, and I was told where I could find you," said I.

"Help, there not be many needin' my help. What is it thee want?"

"I have a responsibility to my aunt; you see she left instructions for me to carry out a *duty* so that her soul could rest in peace after her death," I explained.

"So dead then, is she?"

"Yes, very much so."

"This duty, has somethin' to do with the old curse of Little Childwick I dare say," probed Seth, and it was almost as though he could read my thoughts, however in all probability, it was because he had helped many who had come to his table before.

"It does indeed, you have concluded rightly sir."

"Well, if thee want me to help dig up the old girl, thee must realise that such skulduggery runs the risk of a man being put behind bars."

"You would be doing me a great service and I shall pay you well for your help," I cajoled. Our conversation was suspended as I waited for him to quaff back his ale. He thumped down his empty tankard.

"Let me see the money," he said, and I produced my coin purse and tipped out the contents upon the tabletop. Upon eyeing the glittering sovereigns Seth licked his lips then leaned towards me resting his elbows on the table.

"Where does the old girl lie?" he asked, in a voice no louder than a whisper.

"She is laid to rest at All Hallows cemetery," I confirmed.

"Then I will meet thee at All Hallows tonight, at the hush of midnight," he instructed.

Upon returning to Doyle House, I immediately set to work assembling the talisman. I diligently followed my aunt's instructions. Removing the single infant's shoe from the bedside drawer I placed inside a silver sixpence, a pinch of salt, and one of the acorns I had collected from the deep-rooted landmark that overshadowed and dwarfed all of its own kind. The shoe I then laced tightly and placed the charm into my coat pocket.

After a warm supper, I changed into my old clothes and the rest of the evening I spent busying myself winding the innumerable clocks and firing up the chimneys; anything to avoid the dreadful stillness and ominous expectancy of a recurrence of my dead aunt's spirit. When the clocks pealed the quarter hour past eleven, I pulled on my coat and left the house for the shadows of the night.

My walk to the cemetery was fraught with the thoughts of what Seth had said regarding the possibility of being caught and thrown into the gaol for bodysnatching. I found it hard to imagine lawmen or constables (as they are better known in England) being engaged with guarding boneyards, and especially on such chilly nights. Nevertheless, I thought over the wisdom of what I was about to do especially with my darling wife divided from me by oceans. How would this mission serve her and my unborn child if I were to be kept indefinitely under lock and key?

The tower of All Hallows church was now visible beneath a near full moon quietly silvering its steeple. I carried a dark lantern, and I stopped just inside the lychgate to light the wick. As I held out the light before me, the angel statues scattered amongst the graves took on eerie forms as they stood guarding their plots like a gathering of phantoms.

I saw the silhouette of a spindly man emerge from behind one of the sculptures. He was carrying something and as his face caught the glow from my outstretched lantern, I was glad to see that it was Seth.

"Thee came then?" he said. I nodded. "Never 'ad second thoughts?"

"The job needs doing," said I.

"I will take payment now if you don't mind," demanded Seth, and he held out his expectant hand. "Just in case we are discovered and 'ave to run for it. Thee never knows."

I agreed and handed over my coin purse. Seth pocketed the money then handed me one of the spades he carried.

"Now, which is it?" he asked.

The owls emitted low hoots from their perches high in the treetops and the wind began to rise as I led Seth to my aunt's grave.

"This is the one," I said, pointing at the monument.

"Why, I buried this old girl m'self!" remarked Seth, "The one with the glass window, when all of us poor folk only 'ave to make do with grass windows," he quipped.

Seth set to work using his spade to cut the outline of the grave and in no time had removed the top layer of sod. I joined to help him and the fact that there were the two of us made light work of the task. With the copper flue window removed we both dug down until my spade struck the casket lid. With our hands we cleared the remaining earth from the box; the wood and fixings were still in good order. I carefully undid the thumbscrews and detached the top.

The sight of my aunt's mutilated corpse was almost too much for us to bear. An incredible transformation had taken place since I had first viewed her down the chimney window. The body was badly mangled and what *pulp* still remained had been partially eaten away, particularly around the eye sockets, nose, and the neck. Seth let out a gasp of shock before blessing himself with the sign of the cross. With a handkerchief covering my mouth I stooped to deposit the talisman near to the original that looked as though it had been gnawed. I saw a dried nut protruding from the lace and something upon it glinted under the lantern's light. I do not know what compelled me to reach over and pocket the nut, it was as though for a moment, my reflexes were not my own.

Seth helped pull me out of the hole and after I had straightened and brushed the loose soil from my clothes, I turned in time to witness the dry body of my aunt rattle and her jaw fell slack to release a peculiar and tapered shadow born from the gape and was thenceforth difficult to track with the eyes before it appeared to leap out from the grave towards where we both stood, mutually fixed with mounting terror.

We fell onto our backs as though flattened by a gust of wind. Seth hurled my money purse back at me.

"Keep your money, I ain't takin' it. My God, the woman *is* cursed!" he cried, before fleeing the scene and vanishing into the night. I stood and took up the lantern and scanned the area about where I was. I took a moment to recompose myself and hastily concluded that we must have disturbed an animal (probably a large rat) that had gnawed its way into the casket. Happy enough with my reasoning and glad to see that Seth had abandoned both his shovels, I repositioned the casket lid and with rapidly dwindling courage, I worked hard to cover the grave as best I could. When I had finally replaced the grassy sods, it was not obvious that the grave had been so tampered with other than the chimney window which was now useless. When I was finished, I hid both spades behind a low hedge before making a swift departure.

That night when I had returned to Doyle House, as good luck would have it, I discovered a supply of brandy in the cellar and poured myself a stiff drink, swallowing one or two glassfuls of the potent liquor and began to feel all the better for it. Whilst warming myself near the fire, I remembered the nut I had removed from the coffin, and I pulled it out of my pocket to examine under the firelight. There was something embedded within the seed, and I could now see that it was a barbed tooth, small, yet sharp enough so that I suffered a cut when attempting to pluck it out. I wrapped the nut in a handkerchief placing it back in my pocket before the cheering drink had me slipping into a deep sleep, the first unbroken sleep Doyle House had granted.

***

The visions of my deceased aunt beset me no further, and for that I was glad. However, it had been the way that one plague had been replaced by another. There was now a new and even more disquieting presence within the house. I became beleaguered by the sound of a trilling *caterwauling* that at times I was convinced resembled the breathy wailing of a baby. I searched thoroughly for the cause of the unsettling sound yet try as I might, I could never be in the same space. Whenever I followed the sound, it would cease only to recur in another far-off room. It was not a constant trouble but this made it all the worse because I never knew when my peace would be shattered by this cry from some unseen soul slicing into mine.

VI

I spent more nights with my accommodating neighbours as I counted down the days for my ticketed voyage back across the Atlantic. I never mentioned the new noises that disturbed the peace of Doyle House, for all of Cynthia's enthusiasm for otherworldly curiosities. I did not want them to consider the possibility that they had a lunatic taking up residence beside them. I did however mention the discovery of the singular grave marker at All Hallows that bore my own family name. After the discovery of a similar stone carrying my aunt's name, I conjectured the real possibility that the curse of Little Childwick had somehow been passed on to me. The idea gripped me with growing horror as I spoke of it. Was I now sentenced to fear what next world exists beyond the grave? Could the curse of this town stretch so far across the oceans to infect my own little family back in Copper Hollow?

Cynthia had been a good ear and she said my fears had no foundation because of the good news I had shared with both her and Peter about the condition of Annie. Try as I might, I could not shake off the belief that something had now fastened itself to me and that the longer I remained in Little Childwick, the more I could be adding further linkages to what may become a heavy chain of affliction.

One evening during the middle of the week (and feeling that I had outstayed my welcome at the Inneses') I returned to Doyle House where, after collecting a sledgehammer from a lean-to at the rear of the house (and consuming a fortifying drink of brandy), I took a walk to All Hallows churchyard with the intention of demolishing the singular headstone. That night I did not need to carry a lamp as the full moon with its bright glow became the softest of lanterns to lighten my path.

The bare and twiggy branches above danced as silhouettes against the moonlight, casting their forms upon the slab itself as I stood with the hammer raised wondering if what I was about to do was indeed wise. The first strike cracked the stone and the second shattered it into lumps that spoiled the once clear area that had surrounded it.

I dropped the tool when I heard the first cry, that same infantile wail as heard at the house. I revolved in the darkness and with each twist and turn, searched for the source of the perturbing sound. I stumbled, falling over the rubble at my feet, my head narrowly missing a collision with a large chunk amongst the remains. With my ear almost to the ground I could now hear a man's cry:

"*They are calling him lowborn,*" and then, "*Annie, dear God Annie, help me I am trapped with it!*"

The voice bled through the earth muffled by the sods that roofed it but the words were repeated over and over like an unholy echo, and I recognised the tones as those of my own. When a man works in a mine for most of his life, he becomes familiar with the sound his own voice makes as it ricochets from within the tunnels burrowed into the earth. Mixed with the footsteps and the clattering of unseen almost phantom minecarts, it can be an unsettling experience but nothing could have frightened me more than hearing this disembodied voice calling the name of my wife. I picked myself up and I tore through the churchyard and did not stop running until I had reached Doyle House.

The days that followed my fright at All Hallows were by and large uneventful. The incorporeal wailing about Doyle House had for the most part subsided although I chose to spend as much of my time away from the place as possible, frequenting the local tavern until the wee hours where to my amusement, I became drafted into a team playing *Nine Pins* where the winning prize consisted mainly of ale on the house. I often saw Seth in his corner near to the fire but neither of us ever spoke to the other and he barely looked in my direction so as to avoid catching my eye.

In order to affirm the reality of the haunting cries issuing from beneath the earth, I returned to the spot at All Hallows but choosing to do so in the daytime. The sunlight instead of moonshine was more of a comfort yet during the early onset of winter, the afternoon light was already thinning away. Again with an ear to the ground I could hear my own voice seeping through the turf, and if this itself was not appalling enough, there was also the shocking revelation that the gravestone that I had hammered and ruined had now somehow become whole again and was still emblazoned with my own family name.

Perturbed, I headed into town to spend much trouble hunting down a seller of infant crib shoes. During the search I received many *knowing* looks from other patrons who, after hearing what I sought, would make distance between them and I or depart the store entirely as though I was disease-ridden. Eventually, after managing to acquire the shoes I returned to Doyle House where I constructed a new talisman.

I was invited to dine with my neighbours again as I am sure both had reached the accurate conclusion that I was not eating too well. It was during dinner that I eventually confessed my intentions of digging up the grave that bore my own name and placing within it the new talisman I had made.

"Oh Charles, what a horrid thought! You must reconsider this course of action," implored Cynthia. Peter agreed. "I suggest that you put all of these thoughts out of your mind entirely. Pray, go home to your wife sir, and put distance between you and these fanciful voices from the dead," he said.

"I do intend to return to Copper Hollow in the next few days but beforehand, I am determined to carry out the task that I have set out before you," said I. "I feel I have no other choice."

Both Peter and Cynthia gave me further anguished looks.

"Please Charles, reconsider your intentions. Is there nothing I can say to change your mind?" pleaded Peter, as Cynthia stopped eating to take up his hand.

"Is there nothing I can do to persuade you to help *me*? The task must be carried out covertly and under darkness. I am not sure that I am courageous enough to undertake this alone."

Peter dabbed his lips with a napkin and all three of us became silent as we waited for our dinner crockery to be removed. Once we were alone again with a fresh carafe of wine, it was Peter who spoke first.

"As I explained before, digging up graves is a risky business with harsh penalties for whoever is caught doing so. I am sorry Charles but the best help I can offer you my friend is to convince you to drop the idea entirely."

I sat disheartened knowing that I was committed to the job alone. I thanked both Peter and Cynthia for listening to me and for their frank counsel before I tossed down all the wine my glass held in a single swallow. I declined the offer of a cigar and a seat in my neighbour's drawing room after the clock sang out the late hour. I bade my friends goodnight after making my excuses to depart feigning weariness but having no intention of pillowing my head, not least until after I had revisited All Hallows Church.

I walked through the church yard clothed in moonbeams and collected one of the two spades that still rested behind the hedge where Seth and I had left them. I returned to the plot that was now dominated by the singular headstone now somehow taller as though pushed further up through the earth. My name now seized the moonlight within the deeply cut inscription as though lit from behind.

As I stood contemplating the possible *grave* implications of my next objective, the same haunting, insipid cries from below the turf became audible. I removed my coat placing it over the gravestone, and began digging up the earth whilst the pleads for mercy continued to bleat. I stopped digging periodically because I became aware of another cry, the same shrill squalling that had tormented me back at Doyle House. I stared into the shadows like a frightened animal but could see nothing. *"Annie, dear God Annie, help me I am trapped with it!"* the pleading continued and so did my digging until I was standing in a gaping chasm and the spade hit something firm. I dropped the tool and used my shuddering hands to clear away the last inch or so of dirt from something that looked like a funerary box but unlike any I had seen before. This knotty case as large as a standard adult casket seemed to be the product of something that had *grown* rather than had been built by a coffin maker. It was a fibrous woody tuber of twisted, woven roots and tendrils. There was no distinguishable lid however, although an overhanging lip gave an impression of a cover. I felt the blood turning to ice in my veins as I could still hear the muffled cries from within.

I retrieved the spade and inserted its blade under the lip and with all the strength I could muster, managed to prise open the case. Without hinges, the lid, like a vast clam, attempted to reseal itself and I used the handle of the spade to keep it open so that I could examine the interior. Before I had managed to open the case, my mind had already visualised the horrors that may lie within; a ghoulish apparitor with a face set as a rictus mask from the days, months, or years where it had lain in the darkness grinning at the daisy roots.

The cold moonshine revealed the casket to be mostly empty other than for a piece of grubby cloth. I climbed inside and picked up the cloth that under the cool light I could see, held markings. It was a simple repeated pattern of printed feathers. The flooring underneath the cloth bore nothing but the teeming and writhing bodies of the lice and worms that are known to inhabit all graves.

Without warning, there came a feeling of bristling hairs on the back of my head as an awning of deeply penetrating cold air descended over me extending from the gravestone and filling the cavity in which I stood. With my arms and legs temporarily disabled I remained fixed and rigid as some slice of the night appeared to hover at the edge of the hole. I could see something half childlike and half beast, a lump-covered skull that appeared to be illuminated from within. This elemental leapt from the precipice of the hole I had dug, and its swift movement broke my palsy.

I fell backwards into the casket catching the spade and breaking the prop that had held the lid ajar. The lid snapped shut a mere moment before the vast mound of excavated dirt collapsed and fell back upon the casket sealing me within the cavity. Inside, the musty air became suddenly thin, my eyes were open but everything was as black as the depths of a never-ending mineshaft. It was too snug for me to use my arms against the lid with any advantage, and then, amid the sensation of the crawling bodies of the hordes of mini beasts that violated my skin, I felt the presence of something even more ghastly.

Whatever I had fleetingly witnessed perched atop the edge of the pit was now buried along with me. I could feel its substance as it crawled up my body, claws digging into my flesh, the stench of decay, and the appalling sound of its breathing, snuffling, and infantile gurgling. I was trapped alive with a malignant being of whose origins and intentions I could scarcely imagine, and like my aunt before me, I felt that I was about to suffer death and the torments of the damned, into what life exists beyond the grave. I cried out until I was hoarse, I called to God, I called to my dead parents, and I called for Annie. Finally, I understood that the voice I had perceived when above ground had been my own all along breaking through the barriers of time.

If it is possible to die from fright, then I believe my own demise had been wholly imminent. I even believed that I had already departed the mortal world when I saw a burning bright light and heard a voice calling my name. The sensation of a hand clasping my own and then being dragged upwards and out of the dark humid trap into the frigid night air woke me from my inertia. I coughed and rubbed at my eyes to remove the lingering glare from the lantern that Peter had now set down upon the grass.

"Charles, my God man, if not for your cries I would never have found you alive! Do you prefer the company of the dead to the living?" Peter lambasted.

Once I had collected myself, I thanked him profusely.

"I thought it was the only way, to save my soul," I tried to explain, and feeling stronger I stood and took up the lantern and I held it so that it illuminated our surroundings whilst I searched for a trace of something I remembered clinging to me; the sensation of its clawed limbs still lingered.

"I had the notion that you would be up to something reckless, and I was right to follow you. I came to talk you out of it, and I saw your coat!" he said, pointing at the gravestone.

I put it on and removed the talisman from the pocket.

"This will not save me," said I, and tossed it away.

Looking down into the interlaced woody casing I saw how Peter, during my rescue, had ripped off the lid almost entirely and the 'feathered' cloth lay rumpled inside. I cast the lamp into the hole and its paraffin caused a blaze that consumed everything within. When all was mostly reduced to embers, I wrenched and strained at the gravestone as it appeared almost rooted like a vast tooth. We both managed to twist it loose before pushing it into the smouldering pit. Together, we worked to backfill the hole and afterwards I was relieved when we had passed through the lychgate, as I knew that for me it would be the last and final time that I would ever visit All Hallows.

VII

In the days following that night at All Hallows churchyard there were no further disturbances at Doyle house, yet sleep was as ever elusive. Each time I lay in bed my imaginings instantly cast me back to that unclean hole in the ground and my dreams were filled with nefarious decaying creatures and I never felt as though I was ever truly alone under the coverlets.

I received a new letter from Annie in which she made her feelings clear about leaving Copper Hollow. She said that she had no desire to give up everything she had ever known and leave her home for a new life in England. She implored that I reconsider such a move and gave a convincing argument in favour of us both remaining in Missouri. In truth, I needed no persuasion, and I wrote back to tell her as such and of news of my return.

I quickly set in motion the legal procedures to allow for Doyle House to be sold and for the proceeds to be transferred to a bank in Missouri by means of a bill of exchange. The morning finally came where I bade farewell to my neighbours who surprisingly seemed genuinely sad to hear of my plans to never return, even after all the troubles I had unintentionally laid upon their own doorstep. Afterwards, I took the morning stage to catch a train for Liverpool, whence I departed on the packet with a fair wind back to America.

***

During the voyage home my nights were yet filled with persistent and unsettling nightmares and my days during the long voyage were full of wakeful questions. One night whilst getting dressed for bed I discovered in a pocket of my vest the acorn I had removed from my aunt's grave. The nut still had the tooth lodged and my own fanciful reasoning saw it to be responsible for my bad dreams. If the small porthole in my cabin could open, I would have discarded it there and then but alas this was not possible. Instead, I placed it as far away from the bed as the small berth allowed and planned to dispose of it at the earliest opportunity the following day.

I took the morning stage to catch a train for Liverpool, whence I departed on the packet with a fair wind back to America.

That next morning, I was up and dressed before first light, due as ever to feeling a little *green about the gills*. I denied myself breakfast as had been my current habit and took myself up on deck to brace the squally winds and seize the rails as the ship was tossed about upon waves like rising mountains. As I looked out to sea, I could see nothing but the dark brooding skies and the angry churning brine. It struck me that I and every other soul onboard were completely in the hands of nature. These thoughts gave one a quickening sense of perspective as if not for the ship's compass, all sense of placement and direction would be lost. I now more than ever craved to walk upon the brown soil of home, to embrace Annie, and to lay my weary head upon the pillow of my own bed at our humble abode. Before I left the handrail at the stern, I cast the shrivelled acorn into the sea just as the first clap of thunder cracked through the heavens.

***

Once docked at St Louis I exchanged one vessel for another and rode the steamboat to a port in Missouri and from there boarded a train for Copper Hollow. There followed a walk along a green track and then down a cattle trail that cut through the prairie where our cabin sat. The walk was made all the more pleasant when the fading sun cast its weak light to glitter over the bountiful snow that now blanketed the prairie this late in December. When I saw the cabin appear some way ahead my smile expanded to rival the big skies above and if not for my luggage that felt heavier each instant, I think I would have run all the way over to where that simple, yet homely pile of logs stood with its solitary chimney sending wisps of smoke like twirling dreams skyward.

Annie was taken completely by surprise when she unbolted the door to find me standing on the porch. She was as pleased to see me as I was to be back in her arms. She looked to be full of the health of motherhood and at once, all the anxiety I had carried with me upon the packet as she sailed across the ocean melted away, and was replaced with the happiness that was to come from fatherhood.

The German customs so established in

England had, in recent years, been adopted in the American larger towns of the north and had spilled down into the prairie towns of the south. Evergreen trees were cut down and decorated with strings of nuts, trinkets, oranges, lemons, and candies. The trees were placed around the town of Copper Hollow, and we had a little one of our own at the cabin. We received a Christmas card from Peter and Cynthia, depicting scenes of bountiful Christmas foods, wishing us the joys of the season.

Whilst most folk about town took the occasion to feast, dance, gamble, or visit family, Annie and I remained at home because of her delicate condition and because the weather had declined, bringing further snow to lie deep upon the already crisp land. Our wood stockpile was lower than in previous years due to my absence but there was enough to see us through the winter and the cabin stayed warm and snug.

It was after supper one evening when Annie suddenly began to feel the birthing pains. She collapsed into a chair as she moaned and writhed. We did not possess a horse as we had no stabling, so I had no choice but to leave Annie and to traipse through the thick snow to get to her brother, Shane's place. Shane owned a wagon and he drove it out to fetch the doctor whilst I went back to be with Annie.

After what seemed like an eternity, Shane arrived with Doctor Emmerson and the doctor's wife Nancy. I had put Annie to bed and both Nancy and Shane stayed with me as the doctor saw to Annie. Nancy said that a baby born this early would not survive and was a danger to the mother too, and that I should prepare myself for the worst. We drank two whole pots of coffee before I was called into the loft.

I saw Annie quietly crying into her pillow. I tried to comfort her, and I looked to the doctor for an explanation. Doctor Emmerson was busily wrapping something in the corner of the loft, and he placed down the bundle when he saw me and came over to where I stood. His sleeves were rolled, his brow moist, and he wore a disquieted expression. Before he spoke, he placed a hand upon my shoulder.

"I am sorry Charles, the child did not develop as expected. I am hopeful that Annie will make a full recovery but there is the possibility that she might not be able to bear more children. Annie is a healthy and an honest, God-fearing woman and I will pray for her Charles, for both of you."

I looked past the doctor to the lifeless bundle he had left unattended behind him.

"Our child is dead?" I asked, and as I spoke Annie's crying intensified. The doctor held onto my arm as I tried to go over to where he had left the bundle.

"The child was *lowborn*, and would have been

deformed if it had lived, it was weasel armed and severely cleft. It is nature's way, God's way that it did not."

I broke free and made my way over to the bound wad of cloth. When I saw it, with its delicate repeated pattern of printed feathers I was instantly transported to a murky night at All Hallows cemetery. I did not unwrap the covers. I never looked upon my own dead child trussed in a blanket Annie had bought for the crib. The doctor took it with him to keep at his place until the burial.

VIII

Christmas came and went almost on a side wind. Neither of us paid any mind to the Holy day and my only concern was for Annie and nursing her back to full health. We had a lot of callers at the cabin in the days that followed our loss. The people who came by all meant well but their words only opened wounds that we were trying so desperately to sew up. I made all the arrangements to have our child buried at Clay Cross Cemetery soon after the thaw but nothing prepared us for the sight of the little cross that had been so sympathetically crafted. We never had a name for our child as we never knew the sex. The wooden cross simply said:

OUR ANGEL
BORN SLEEPING

As the small box was lowered into the ground, I could hear the whispered comments spoken by folks around the graveside, '*Imperfect*', '*Freak*', '*Lowborn*'. I knew that Annie could hear it too so I held her hand tightly and tried to hold her close to me but she had grown distant of late, as though she blamed me for all our hurt. The only people she allowed to comfort her were her old family but I cared not as all I wanted was for her to be consoled, and I hoped that soon she would return to me to fill the gap between us that felt as cold as a grave.

As we listened to the compassionate words of the preacher, I turned to the spot where an old elm grew, and the preacher's words became muted to my ears. A bitter wind ruffled my coat and time stood still as my eyes fell upon a crooked gravestone that rested at the base of the tree almost leaning against it. I left Annie's side and made my way over largely unnoticed by the small congregation.

I knelt to view the childlike inscription that covered its face, the same scrawl produced by the same hand as I had seen in All Hallows Cemetery. *BURYMAN*, it read simply. Around the stone grew winter heliotrope, the mauve blooms that smell like cherry pie, each adorned with dewdrops that rolled off the flower and down the stem like mournful tears. I reached out to touch the stone but withdrew my hand before contact was made. I was repelled by it, and I stood and backed away from the elm as I recalled my homecoming as I had crossed the prairies with a heart bursting with the keenness of a reunion with Annie.

Before I had walked the trail to the cabin, I had seen the small spire of the church at Clay Cross Cemetery. My hands were cold, and I swapped the carrycase from one to the other and dug the empty hand deep into my coat pockets and it was then I discovered the acorn complete with its embedded fang. I pondered if days of seasickness and delirium through lack of sleep had woven a false memory where I believed that I had cast the nut from the ship's handrails. There was no other rational explanation to how, after ridding myself of it, the thing was still upon my person. In my haste to finally purge myself of the article I digressed from the trail homeward and wandered into Clay Cross Cemetery. There I jabbed a hole under the tall elm and pushed the acorn into the ground. It seemed to be a fitting place to bury *Time's Tooth* that had gnawed away at Annie's and my soul. I now knew that the grave at All Hallows was never a foreshadow of my own grave as I had once thought, but the grave of my infant child.

The author would appreciate an Amazon and Goodreads review.

I do read all the reviews each and every one and I am very grateful to anyone who has taken the time to post a review. I appreciate the time you have taken reading this book. I hope you enjoyed reading it as much as I enjoyed writing it.

You are welcome to join David on his Facebook page and group where you can receive news about forthcoming releases, and to discuss and share thoughts and queries about any of David's published works.

www.facebook.com/davidralphwilliams

Have you also read:

Sacred – Ghostly Tales.

Three traditional Victorian ghost stories.

For many, the ghost stories of old and particularly, from our Victorian forebears have always been popular. The Victorians excelled at telling them as they had an uncanny flair for capturing the feeling of malevolence and unearthly horror. Christmas eve has traditionally been the time to tell such frightening and eerie stories whilst seated around the fireside. Montague Rhodes James a principal of King's College Cambridge was a master of this art and would invite students and friends to his chambers each Christmas eve to listen in whilst he read to them one of his much-celebrated ghost stories.

I have been fortunate myself to have dined within the walls of King's College near the time of Christmas and have tried to absorb what residual atmosphere remains from these times of old. Thus, as in the great man's tradition I invite you to curl yourself around my hearth (metaphorically speaking) and allow me to tell you a ghost story, or three as it happens from within the pages of this book.

Don't be perturbed by tales of old country houses where malicious spirits linger and may, as one art curator discovers, become attached especially after removing something that is sacred to them.

Try not to dismiss the folklore of devils and other unclean spirits while working alone in solitude like my artisan of stained-glass attempts to do while trying to piece together the fragments of a broken window that once adorned an old sacred tower.

And under no circumstances ignore warnings of curses that surround infamous lost treasures as some things have remained lost for very good reasons.

Remain calm and take deep breaths because these new ghosts of Christmases past are gathering and are ready for you to discover them.

The following passage is taken from Sacred – Ghostly Tales:

As I unhooked the painting from its nail, I heard a sound from behind me, a gentle rumpling. Holding the portrait, I turned and saw a looking glass on the wall opposite. The glass had been covered by a mourning cloth, and the wrap had partially slipped down. I carried the painting over to the looking glass and I removed the mourning cloth and used it to wrap up the picture; the cloth would suffice as a protective cover against the elements outside as I carried it back to the station. One of the windows in the room had the remnants of a set of heavy, velvet drapes. There was a pull-cord dangling and frayed and I ripped it down and used it to fasten the cloth around the painting more securely.

Happy with my handiwork, I turned to leave the room but stopped firm in my stride when a casual glance again towards the looking glass revealed something indiscernible, shifting, and constantly redeploying itself upon the reflective surface. I rubbed at my eyes and tried to focus on the anomaly, now coalescing into – a form. I turned around to examine the wall behind but the figure in the glass was not a reflection of something in the room, it was it seemed, inhabiting the glass itself. I stood rigid with fright as slowly, and nimbly the figure climbed out from the looking glass, its lengthy cadaverous frame dropping to the floor. It crouched momentarily squat and hunched, with its face turned away from me, and then it seemed to uncurl itself as it straightened. It wore the clothes of a gentleman, although now outdated, and the apparel was old, ragged, and fusty. This impossible spectacle was akin to something experienced, I imagined, when under the effect of opioids. Finally, it turned and regarded me where I stood, paralysed by my fear.

It had a wrinkled, thin corpse-like face, pinched and trailing down to a tapered chin. Its mouth was a mere pinhole and yet it dripped a rancid slime as it sucked and blew out air as it sought to breathe. The thing had an unruly mop of black hair and it appeared to float about the head as though I was observing it underwater. It was a ghastly sight and I recoiled in horror of it. It looked at me full in the face. It was a terrible gaze. I must confess that I quailed under it, for it was a malevolent stare, full of hatred. With uplifted twitching hands, it advanced towards me.

The Christmas Room

To Arabella, Star Lake Hall was a cold name for a house and it conjured up images of cool dark waters sprinkled with the reflections of ancient suns. The old rambling country house was filled by memories of the past that had become locked away inside as though frozen in time.

Newly married and now living at Star Lake Hall she soon becomes fascinated by old stories involving the disappearance of her husband's late uncle Laurence.

Warned to let old ghosts rest she nevertheless continues in her quest to find answers and by doing so it is not long before the old memories sealed within the house become interested in her.

After a lifetime of dreams about Star Lake Hall she soon realises that her whole life has been leading up to the day she entered through its doors, and particularly, through a door to one special room.

The following passage is taken from The Christmas Room:

Anyone who has ever experienced being seized by a *ghost* in a dream will tell you how fearful they are of being in the presence of one after they have woken. The sensation of the cold hands wrapping themselves around my own in the dream was so powerful that when I woke with a jolt, I could feel that I was under the watchful gaze of another's *presence* in the room. I sat up in my bed and called out.

"Who's there?"

Nobody answered and neither did I expect an answer because dreams, when broken do not answer, or so I thought.

Before I went to sleep, I had left the window

uncovered so that I could search for the pair of stars that Claude had likened to our twin souls shining brightly within the night sky. The moonlight had flooded my room and had come to rest at the foot of the bed. I could now see the shape of a child as she stepped out of the gloom and her dark eyes cast an icy gaze upon me. Her face was caught under the moonlight reflecting a shadow-daubed, marble white pallor. Her tissue thin skin was stretched across her skull forming creases that resembled the fine lines often seen upon the faces of porcelain dolls. She glided effortlessly away from my bed and towards the door where she beckoned with a clandestine signal and although terrified, I was compelled to follow.

David Ralph Williams has been writing traditional ghost stories for many years. David has written six previous books of ghost stories and is co-author of the Paranatural Detective Agency adventures. His new book, *Three Ghosts of Christmas* and his previous works, *The Christmas Room*, and *Sacred – Ghostly Tales*, are inspired by his love of traditional ghost stories, particularly by the works of MR James and Susan Hill and the BBC's tradition of televised ghost stories for Christmas. David currently lives in Cheshire in the UK.

Printed in Great Britain
by Amazon